The Females

The Females

Wolfgang Hilbig
Translated by Isabel Fargo Cole

TWO LINES
PRESS

Originally published as *Die Weiber*, *Alte Abdeckerei*, *Die Kunde von den Bäumen* by Wolfgang Hilbig, Werke, Erzählungen © 2010, S. Fischer Verlag GmbH, Frankfurt am Main

Translation © 2018 by Isabel Fargo Cole

Two Lines Press
582 Market Street, Suite 700, San Francisco, CA 94104
www.twolinespress.com

ISBN 978-1-931883-76-4

Library of Congress Control Number: 2018948090

Cover design by Gabriele Wilson
Cover photo by Millennium Images/Adrian Muttitt
Typeset by Jessica Sevey

Printed in the United States of America

1 3 5 7 9 10 8 6 4 2

This project is supported in part by an award from
the National Endowment for the Arts.

ART WORKS.
arts.gov

The translation of this work was supported by a grant from
the Goethe-Institut.

GOETHE
INSTITUT

Other titles by Wolfgang Hilbig available
from Two Lines Press

The Tidings of the Trees
Old Rendering Plant
The Sleep of the Righteous

It was hot, a damp hot hell, sweat emerged from all my pores. I began excreting smells, how strange, as though something within me were starting to mold, an extraordinary *fromage*, as though I smelled of my eyeballs, which bulged and welled with what seemed a sort of slime, a turbidity likely rising up from my loins, a twinge from the groin that brushed my heart, stinging; it dug slowly into my brain, but I hadn't felt its onset. — I'd become unfit for the tool shop, and was sent down to the basement to arrange steel casting molds and cutting tools on the shelves, neatly and cleanly, as I was told. Cleanly—but wherever my moist hands touched the molds, rust appeared a few days later. During inspections these spots earned me reprimands, and I began to brush the molds with oil, oil that sizzled on the brown surfaces, emitting a burned smell; but stronger by far was the smell

I myself emitted. Great flaking scabs infested my elbows, white eruptions that smelled of sour milk, and I hunkered inert at the table in the humid basement, not even shocked but dismayed to see all my fears confirmed with such absurd consistency, all my thoughts turned almost purposefully into stagnant poison. — Daily, and later several times a day, I masturbated in the basement, treading that shimmering spittle across the concrete floor; there was not the slightest reason for these abuses, not even a physical urge; you swine, I told myself, hurry up, or someone will walk in on you. But it took me longer and longer; I whipped myself into increasingly harried states, but the twinge from my hips never faded; meanwhile I went on sweating, outpourings that paralyzed and weakened me, my member drained my last remaining strength, and when I shook myself with my weary fist I spluttered out nothing but a dry, painful cough. — I went on sweating, though the windowless basement, lit by a single light bulb, seemed cooler than the air of those three summer months smoldering outside the factory.

A bit more light fell through a square grate in

one corner of the ceiling; it came from the pressing shop above the basement, where the machines
pounded away. Much earlier, when this factory
had produced munitions, using prisoners from the
camp directly attached to it, valuable metal filings
had been dumped into the basement through this
grate. Now it served as the hatchway for a mechan-
ical hoist that lowered the often extremely heavy
molds—which I dismantled, cleaned, reassembled,
and gave labels and numbers—from the pressing
shop. But no one would open the grating for me;
left open for hours unattended, they said, it would
be too dangerous for the women who worked in the
pressing shop and had to walk back and forth past
it. I dragged the molds down to the basement via
circuitous routes and steep stairways, which took
days at a time. Following these bouts, I wouldn't
touch a thing at first; I'd sit still at the table, tensely
attending to the tremble of my musculature, the
quiver of my lungs, signals that quieted only gradually; the tools' sharp edges had chafed my hips and
sweat burned fiercely in the wounds, which seemed
to sink deep into my body, as though my nerve cords

were injured, the currents of my senses severed.

And the pressing shop was where the females worked. — Through the grating above me, damp, smoldering heat flooded down with steady force. I sat on a chair beneath the grate amid this hot tide, hidden in semidarkness, several bottles of beer by my chair; when I drank, the beer seemed to gush instantly from all my pores, lukewarm, not even changing temperature inside my body. It was a ceaseless strain— head constantly tilted back—to stare through the grate into the light, always hoping to see the women up there step across the bars. Sometimes I climbed onto the chair, almost touching the iron grid with my brow, to gain a narrow, densely crisscrossed view into the pressing shop; I could see the short stepladder, a bit more than a yard high, by which the women reached the capacious hopper of a mill that ground away with a terrible racket, reducing scraps of cooled plastic—left from the casting of coil-like radio parts in the presses—to granules fine enough for reuse.

From that vantage point I could see two or three women, the oldest and strongest, who were assigned to work the hand presses. Backs turned toward me, they sat on tall three-legged stools that swayed and seemed to squeak; due to the heat they dispensed with cushions, the mass of each gigantic behind completely swallowing the stool's round wooden seat; like all the women in the shop, they wore nothing but thin brightly colored smocks, and when they thrust themselves upward to the presses' long levers I saw that their smocks were hiked up, that they sat back down with parted legs, and that their knees finally tilted inward as their bare or clog-shod feet pressed down on the ends of the long, wide pedals to lock the molds in place; their behinds rose ten inches above the seat and for a moment their thighs seemed to slacken, their buttocks to sag, then tensing to utmost firmness, perhaps pressing intensely fragrant substances into the taut fabric of their smocks; the women—of whose upper bodies I could see only a narrow strip above the waist, since a crane track that crossed the hall spoiled much of my view—had seized in both fists the upward-tilting levers and brought them down by latching on with all their heavy bodies' weight, doing this, I sensed, with deep sighs, as though a log had been split in their chests; the machine's top part then sank down onto the firmly fixed jaws of the mold, discharging a portion of the boiling, steaming plastic; the women, remounting their seats, held down the phallus-like lever so that the plastic released from the nozzles could cool as their thighs gripped the seat's hard surface; I knew that the women's upper arms had stiffened to iron, that their shoulder muscles, shoulder blades, and clavicles had fused into one hard, armored form; then their fists, already drained of blood, let the levers spring back up to open the jaws and eject the two or three cooled coils from the molds' laps. All this was the work of no more than thirty seconds. The women were paid by the piece, and the crew at the hand presses constantly changed, so that throughout the week I could watch nearly all the older women as they worked these machines— always women of similar stature, of similar heft and strength, all similarly dressed, with the damp fabric of their smocks stretched to breaking over the swells and bulges of their prodigious bodies—and often I saw them blur in the fumes of their effluvia, their backs' brightly flowered expanses spilling into the shimmering air of those three summer months that, in the cloud-core of the pressing shop, were nothing but a seething stench of rubber and plastic. — Under their stools I noticed big dark puddles; I speculated that they had formed from the women's sweat or even their urine, but soon surmised resignedly that it was merely the worthless residue of the cooling water trickling from leaky joints in the molds, which the women, unresisting, allowed to bathe their legs.

Now and then men stepped lightly across the grating above my brow, the men from the tool shop, moving elegantly, wearing almost spotless uniforms, holding delicate, harmless tools; their job was to ensure that the machines ran smoothly, and quickly perform minor repairs, strutting unperturbed through the racket, fanning themselves, chatting near the ventilators; none of them heeded the lewd, uncouth remarks the women yelled in their direction over the hiss of the presses, the pounding of the machinery, the howling of the mills, the crunch of the cutting tools, through the whole rhythmically gathering and splitting fabric of noise—remarks I heard clearly, but did not understand.

The women never crossed the grate. Rarely, unexpected and quick as a flash, they'd skim some little corner of my vision: alas, they passed in twos or threes without ever setting a clog on the iron lattice, their shadows barely flitting over me; for a fraction of a second I'd hear their voices, an incomprehensible, indistinguishable chatter; they were contourless cylinders of darkness, speechless silhouettes wafting across me; all I could see were the objects they carried, pressed to their hips: large, evidently heavy cardboard boxes which alone could be clearly discerned hovering over the grate. I wouldn't see the women again until they stopped at the stepladder by the waste mill. This was the long-awaited moment when I'd press my brow, my face against the grate to see—to see one of the two women climb the stepladder to lean forward over the mill hopper, at which I'd fail to notice a third woman following the first two with a bucket in her hand. It was the moment when the hem of the smock worn by the forward-leaning woman on the ladder seemed to slip far up the reddened backs of her thighs, when the smock's flimsy synthetic fabric seemed to blaze

in the light of the nearby window, in that white-
hot thrust of sunlight; the moment when the heavy,
slightly gaping buttocks must be revealed instantly,
as if through some trick of physics in an incalcula-
ble second, soon, instantly, exposing a point of invisible darkness, the lightning-like moment when a
hot drop of sun must inflame the nerves of the flesh
that would be freed—I had no idea what I meant by
that—and the moment in which the third woman
following the other two indulged in a savage jest,
doubtless repeated a hundred times over: with a
mighty swing of her arms she tossed the contents of
the bucket, five or six liters of cold clear water, in one
sharp, perfectly calculated jerk of unthinkingly per-
fect aim, sending the water in a beeline through the
burning air and under the smock of the woman on
the ladder, right between the woman's thighs, slap-
ping the entire backside of the woman's lower body,
at which a shriek of amusement from the woman on
the ladder immediately confirmed her most grateful
acceptance—anticipated, but still startling—of the
unerring bull's-eye: *oh what welcome coolness!*; I saw
nothing, I saw the surge of water rebound in spray;

what I'd wanted to see was swamped, washed away and warped by water; as the water coursed to the ground, shot toward the grate and spilled into the basement through the iron lattice, I leaped from my chair to capture it with my cupped hands, which could not catch it, with my face, instantly spattered, with my nose, with my gaping mouth, as though I could grasp some trace—some barely perceptible bloom of femininity that might have been washed off and carried along, that, for all the rapidity of the incident, must have infiltrated the water a tiny bit— grasp it, devour it, retain it in a single pore of my skin, even if I never noticed. Nothing met my lips but dust washed from the floor, nothing clung to my hands but the fouled water's gasoline smell, all I had in my nostrils was the burned-rubber smell, the inhuman smell of plastic which, cooled for a few seconds by the water, now tasted even more vivid and more obscene.

I had gradually begun to transform into a sickness. Like all things I produced, this transformation was utterly excessive; an agony not quite human, it was no longer that of an animal, either. It led to my dismissal from the factory, though the details aren't worth mentioning; I lived in circumstances in which the symptoms outweighed the causes, or, rather, the causes kept transforming into the symptoms; I hid in my apartment by day and went out only at night, in the dark, roaming the town's deserted streets, soliloquizing, holding rousing speeches to myself, sweating, covered with milky green pustules. A terrible thing had occurred, the worst thing ever to have happened since I'd learned to contemplate life from the outside, since I'd learned to use life to manufacture descriptions which made an inner life possible for me. A terrible thing, yet I was supposed to call it beauty. If I'd managed anything like it before…I'd always doubted I could…the discrepancy this time was most stark, it was appalling, nothing about the event could be transformed into a beautiful idea for my inner life. Earlier, I hadn't minded making filth glitter; in earlier writings that I'd submitted for publication—that I'd submitted…I grinned…to *pressure*, or removed from myself in some other way, or that had been removed from me—the horrors had at least been palatable; I'd cloaked them in cheap mystification, and though I'd never been able to establish them on the market, at least their sale was being discussed. Oh, these lovely prisons—in words like these I'd described the trash cans on the street, described them not quite as useful, but as reflectors of magical moonlight, I'd made them gleam in the sun like big tins, I'd called their glitter *silver*.

But now something had happened that I couldn't so easily bend to my will, not any sort of defilement, but rather a lack of richness, an especially painful loss; the town seemed to have suddenly shed a certain part of its makeup; at first I thought it had shed one of its smells. The insanity must have begun the day I was let go from the factory; since that day, at least, I'd felt the lack of some particular thing: venturing out in the evening I struggled for air, it was as though the air were drained of a special aroma, an aroma I needed in order to live. I sought the cause of this sensation; then came a suspicion that grew stronger, and soon I roamed for days at a time just to see how right I was, for nights at a time just to confirm my hideous suspicion: *all the females had vanished from town.* — It was no help at all to sense I was possessed by an obsession, in my overpotent head a cascade of letters blazed: all the females of the species had vanished from town, and with them had fled every trace of femininity. — Not only that, I felt that even feminine nouns had fallen out of use; I thought I suddenly noticed people in town referring to trash cans as *der Kübel* instead of *die Tonne*. When I saw those trash cans from afar, set up in long rows along the curbs that summer—something unlikely to change, as the trash collection service was still more dysfunctional then than in the winter—at first I'd think a line of unshapely females was loitering there, dully iridescent in the bluish streetlights, and I'd hurry toward them. I'd realize they were just the trash cans I saw every night, from their gaping orifices hung rubbish that looked hairy, that had some indefinable evil about it. I went so far as to impetuously embrace a trash can and lift it from the ground, as one sometimes does in the first ardent moments of reunion—that was possible at this time of year, when the containers generally held nothing but rotten fruit and crumpled paper, perhaps some old clothes—and confirmed that what I embraced was a cool, ugly bin of smeary metal that repelled me; I set it back on the ground with a crash and was surrounded by flies that had been resting in the rubbish of the containers and suddenly seemed to regard me as a better place, but then flew away in outrage when I snatched at them.

All the same, I often lingered near those trash cans; in a town like this, I thought, it's from just such a receptacle that a woman, like foam-born Aphrodite, might emerge and rise into the light.

There had never been the least portent of the scandalous debacle I'd witnessed ever since I'd been let go: the disappearance of the females, I thought, must have happened swiftly: a radical, smoothly executed move, a hush-hush operation that met with no resistance; perhaps they'd vanished voluntarily and in unison; it was as though they'd dissolved into thin air, blown away by a wind I hadn't noticed. Most likely it had happened the day I fled the factory in hideous confusion; that evening, upon entering the town—which for me was like returning to a place I'd believed lost—I'd immediately felt that the facts no longer corresponded with my memory, I smelled it with a hyena's keen instinct. I asked myself if their disappearance bore a causal relation to my return, had they felt threatened by my increased opportunities to wander freely through the streets, had I frightened or repulsed them in some other way, had my arrival in town simply made them dissolve, couldn't they tolerate the substance I was made of, was I some sort of antimatter to their matter? Was it just that I could no longer see…hear…smell them? I still had back in the factory, a so-called women's factory employing only a few male specimens…unless I was mistaken. I was no longer sure whether I wasn't mistaken on that point, whether even in the factory I'd ceased seeing, ceased discerning the women. For weeks I had hardly any doubt that *I* bore the blame for their flight, that what I called my return to outward life was, in their eyes, too monstrous an insult. But what about me was it? Was it the prospect of my ubiquitous threatening tirades that had scared them off; was it my appearance, my now-uncontrollable discolorations, the fact that I was growing darker and darker? Was it my lechery, some devious lust that excited me until I realized that it had no foundation, that I lacked the strength to make its ideas into reality? Was it my craving that repelled them, the smell of my dry craving, the thirst to see them constantly, to have them nearby; was it my hand, long since atremble with the inability to touch, even brush one of theirs? Was it my avarice, which made me collect their discarded tissues? Was it the noise of my gullet when draining my bottles? Was it the noise of my lashes, sinking the moment their fleeting gaze grazed me? Was it that I stood out by trying so doggedly to fade into the background? Oh, was it the howling that racked me at night when, with no hope of seeing a single one of them, I crept back to my room; was it my rabidity they sensed?

Of course, it might have been the other way around—perhaps I had disappeared and they, not I, were still present. Perhaps I couldn't see them because I was gone, nonexistent, devoured, hidden in the bowels of my own crab lice, which could find no nest in their cool cleanliness. Or I was hidden in the bowels of my mother...

Perhaps there had, in fact, been a harbinger of this scandalous turn of events. I recalled my lasting alarm over an incident the previous winter. Very early one morning I was sitting in a bus from A. to M., one of the first on that route; it was packed with workers heading to the early shift, and the only free seat was the one next to me. It went unclaimed, though people were even standing in the aisle between the seats. It was neither chance nor delusion; quite clearly they were refusing to sit next to me. Indeed, I looked as though the sickness were already upon me, as though I already were a sickness; yet I knew it hadn't quite seized me, I expected it that coming summer, though I couldn't yet guess its symptoms. Now I interpreted things as follows: on a weekend trip during which everything in my life had gotten mixed up and I hadn't slept for two or three nights, I'd been transformed into a hollow-eyed, feverishly glowing ruin; staggering around, I paraded a dull, glimmering fog that emanated from my face's pale gray skin, a foul-smelling fog that rose from my mouth's burning cavity and from my unwashed armpits. — On the seat just in front of me sat a girl, a young woman, separated from me by the seat back that rose in front of my face and smelled of its green plastic upholstery; the young woman had mounted the bus just before me, gazing about sleepily, infinitely lovely. Her characteristic feature, I'd noticed immediately, was the sharp kink in her nose, bent slightly to the left; either some terrible accident had broken its bridge, or it was due to her harelip, surgically repaired and almost completely smoothed away, a very slight irregularity, but apparently reason enough for the younger man next to her to move as far away as possible. That young man, casually dressed and clearly smelling much less foul than I, worked as a so-called dispatcher in a department of my factory that supervised the tool shop, so that broadly speaking he was one of my superiors; now, fortunately, it seemed he hadn't noticed or hadn't recognized me. His name was exactly the same as mine, which often made people mistake him for me, or rather me for him; the girl, who also worked at our factory, though not in the pressing shop, spoke to him a few times, very quiet words I couldn't understand—she addressed him familiarly

by his first name, that much I understood; of all the
words she said, I heard only the softly lisped name
that was mine, and that sounded wondrous to me
coming from her lips—but he gave no reply, hardly
deigning to look at her. I was firmly resolved that at
the next opportunity, on some pretext, I'd smash his
nose with a blow of my fist—this intention, albeit as
a purely verbal offense, really did play a role in my
dismissal from the factory six months later. — She
seemed to have abandoned the attempt to talk to
him, and leaned her head back against the seat; her
long dark hair, in several smooth spills, hung down
over the upholstery toward me, and after a sharp
curve I noticed that my hand, feeling the need to
brace me, had grabbed the seat and lingered there.
My hand had come to rest just half an inch beside
that hanging hair, resting there without touching it
at all. I glanced around the bus for fear that someone might have noticed the hand's telltale position.
I needed to move it just half an inch to touch the
girl's hair, and probably she wouldn't even feel it. I
didn't move the hand; the hand didn't move. Spellbound and despairing, I froze in the conviction that

it could only be a touch that, on a normal person's skin, would elicit at most a trifling tickle, at most the suspicion of a tickle, so light and delicate…really, no normal person would mind refraining from such a touch; really, such a touch wouldn't even cross their mind. My heart began to flutter, the idea needled me down into my lower extremities, an uncontrollable nervousness, and as a result…I thought I saw my hand twitch, the crippling urge to instantly hurdle that one half inch pulsing unmistakably in my fingers…as a result my entire arm turned to stone and, despite all the willpower I could muster, remained immobile…as a result I had no choice but to grasp without hesitation, to blindly grab those strands of hair that would jerk the young woman's head around in my direction, so that our gazes would suddenly lock, suddenly my gaze would strike in the midst of her face's misfortune, suddenly the name that must linger behind her brow would be spoken to its true, sole bearer…or I'd find the hair was a wig, I guessed it, I saw it, this immobile hand would tear at a sham, in my hand this hair would transform into synthetics, these frozen artificial fingers would touch only the cold, unfeeling tresses of a perfectly manufactured wig…my hand, gone pale, in a white frenzy, as if assuming the fanatical hue of my sleep-deprived face, did not move in the slightest. There was a thought in this hand that wounded me deeply; in this hand was the terrible suspicion that the darkly gleaming, soft, fragrant hair before me, however clearly I saw it, did not really exist.

My losses accumulated: it seemed I'd even lost my name; yes, I no longer knew who I was, my name was the property of a strange personage, that alone put it in the presence of the females, and they suspected nothing. My name was lost, as all that flowing, rustling hair was lost to me…it was lost because I was forbidden to touch it, ah, it was beyond saving. — As we approached the town of M., the bus drove past sprawling garbage dumps, veritable pyramids of trash looming from a landscape of old, filled-in strip mines; dump trucks, engines howling with the effort, scaled the mountainsides of trash until they finally found a place to disgorge themselves, giving one last ghastly howl as they tipped the loads from their orange-red bellies. Eddies of wind snatched at the cargo and whirled it upward…and I had the sense that prodigious quantities of hair were being hurled upon the heaps, I imagined that colossal bales of matted hair in all different hues were being exposed to the weather; oh, I saw hair smoking upon the plain, cloudy skeins of it drifting toward the last bare trees, where they snagged in crippled winter branches to flutter like black scraps of flags, flags to mourn the murderous traditions of my homeland. Trembling with horror, I got off the bus when it stopped at a path that led to a village. I was suddenly nauseous and cold with sweat; with rending intensity I was beset by a thought that put me in a panic, a thought inexplicable to me, yet of the irrevocable veracity one experiences only in the grip of an obsessive suspicion when the whole world around seems to turn into evidence confirming it. It all came back to me: almost exactly a year before, when, out of work in M., I spent several months living on my savings and struggling to use the jobless phase for a writing project—envisioned as a romantic novella with a tragic ending, an experiment meant for myself alone, since I knew I'd never let myself share a manuscript with such an embarrassing subject—I was surprised by a summons from the Workforce Steering Office in the district capital, where I was asked to explain why I hadn't held a regular job for some time. I stammered, I couldn't come up with a convincing excuse; the threatening undertone in the voice of my hefty female interrogator disconcerted and exposed me before I'd even opened my mouth, and all explanations seemed pointless except for the one that would show my true colors. The woman's eyes, fixed upon me, took on a shimmer of mockery and outrage as I began a laborious account of the literary proclivities that had governed me since my youth, and which I felt it was my mission in life to pursue… — Oh, she said, what on earth do you plan to write…?—a question that immediately silenced me… You don't even have a high-school diploma, no…indeed, she said, you didn't even finish tenth grade. But we've offered you the chance to learn a very decent profession…which you've already given up. Your sense of gratitude toward our state and society leaves much to be desired; in fact, it's practically criminal. You want to be an artist…what on earth do *you* plan to write…a writer, but you shy away from facing real life. That's where I have an excellent suggestion for you. As I'm sure you know, the sanitation department in M. is dealing with a considerable shortage of manpower. Trash collection, that's a crucial field of work—aren't they constantly looking for young people? You're young and pretty sturdy. You don't want to work in your profession, which is unfortunate, but you're a pretty sturdy fellow, and the work there isn't for sensitive souls. You should report to them as quickly as possible… — I nodded and promised to follow her advice, but she could tell I was lying: Fine, you do that…meanwhile I'll register you, so we can keep an eye on you and make sure you don't get stuck on the wrong track. —

I didn't know whether I was recalling the speech verbatim. That was beside the point…it seemed as though I'd wished to be attacked in some still more dangerous form: panic filled me, and to contain it I struggled to repeat the woman's speech in every detail, mentally amplifying the vehemence of her statements; if one of the arguments aimed against me seemed too weak, I tried to improve it until its keenness actually wounded me to the quick. I let her speech knife through my mind—while pacing up and down in a panic by the icy, rain-lashed trash heap, and later while walking toward town, the next bus not being due for another two hours or so—and I suddenly realized that the crucial point for me was neither the inanity nor the malice of what I'd heard, but the fact that it was a woman, not a man, who had spoken to me like that. Had it been a man, I could quickly have chosen to take the accusation as a mere insult, I could have replied in kind; ah, I could have laughed about it and forgotten the whole thing as soon as I left the building. The accusations seemed to become a real threat only because they came from a woman's mouth, with a cold impassivity against which I was powerless, with a stony resolve that relegated me to the trash.

The injury caused by the woman's words, an injury I could not separate from the fact that a woman's mouth inflicted it, shielded me all the same—with the very cruelty of the injury—from the naked recognition that it was the state that had *an eye on me*, it was the state, with its ability to punish, that believed I was *on the wrong track.*

If I ever managed to feel that I possessed an identity, if I was able to develop any nebulous ideal of my *I*, it was only through experiencing myself, in writing, as an active subject, albeit a subject I never dared disclose in public: I had made that mistake at the labor office, and my *I* had instantly been rebuffed in the harshest conceivable fashion. For the bureaucrat my *I* was not even a valid category, for her it went without saying that in the form presented to her it had no right to exist whatsoever. She hadn't even explicitly threatened me with forced labor—for that I would have had to be a subject worth reforming in a labor camp—but her words made it more than clear that the option was being kept open. Here, fortunately for my addled mind, I could indulge in a simple projection: that I was faced with the perfectly ordinary hostility of a woman toward an apparently feckless man; I was someone who didn't work, who made no provisions for the future, who might be living at his family's expense, with all the unpleasant social consequences that entailed, and, on top of it all, I gave myself erratic intellectual airs. I was all too familiar with this uncomprehending attitude from my mother—when my mother heaped reproaches on me for my fecklessness and laziness, she rationalized her disappointment with her fear that I'd end up in a labor camp someday. — At this thought I actually seemed to feel a touch of warmth and calmed down for a few moments; the monotonous drone of the bus motor sent me into a light slumber.

My compulsion, later on, to get off at this stop was prompted by another thing, though ultimately it served as an equally inadequate explanation: at some point, ages ago, maybe in the early 1960s, I'd produced a manuscript I then lost later on. Its existence was an incredible embarrassment to me, and I'd so thoroughly mislaid, misplaced, repressed, forgotten it that if it had suddenly reappeared, I'd easily have claimed I hadn't written it, and perhaps I'd even have believed that claim myself. That winter a year in the past, returning home from A. to M. after my summons to the labor office and nodding off in the bus—asleep perhaps for only a minute—I dreamed of that manuscript, which must have shaken my faith in myself, and in myself as a writer. In the dream, I was horrified to see the notebook I thought contained the sorry piece of work some distance from me on a broad desk or judge's bench, behind which people in dark disguises held proceedings against me. The charges were unintelligible, read out in a woman's voice, undoubtedly the voice of the bureaucrat in the office I'd just left, and naturally bearing a strong resemblance to my mother's: the most aggravating circumstance, annihilating me morally, was judged to be the existence of the manuscript that lay on the desk for all to see, which I, in agony, had to recognize as my own, and which I vainly tried to seize, thus revealing myself once and for all as its author...they must even have misunderstood me so drastically as to think I insisted on retaining possession of it. — When the bus stopped for a little more than half a minute at the edge of the garbage dump, I'd woken from the dream with a start; dazed, sweating, racked with horror, I tried to get my bearings; outside, the wind and rain whirled up great quantities of scattered paper scraps that whipped across the road in front of the bus—and at the moment the bus started up again, a page from a notebook, torn nearly in half, momentarily stuck to the window in front of my face, a page from the elementary school exercise books I'd used for years, with writing in green ink in an immature hand which I seemed to clearly recognize as my own from earlier days. It was a hallucination; I thought I could even decipher parts of the text; seized by craven dismay, I persuaded myself that it was a fragment from that childishly obscene story that had vanished, that I'd forgotten...suddenly the text came back to me, a shameful foray into pornography I'd written for myself...the paper blew away, the bus was moving, I couldn't get out now. Perhaps, of course, I'd merely succumbed to an illusion, but it was a fact that my past contained a piece of writing so repugnant, repugnant due solely to my being its author; the dream had recalled that to me all too vividly, it could no longer be denied. — It was a nightmare, a hallucination, but it was enough to make me search like a madman for those compromising old pages as soon as I got home; I couldn't find them, though I dragged out the oldest bundles of papers from the most obscure corners. I made another nasty discovery: at some point my mother seemed to have moved old papers of mine from one place to another—ancient, idiotic texts I'd thought I'd burned long ago—and I was convinced I'd find the pornographic pages among them…but I didn't.

I had long since forgotten what was in that old, lost work. — Later, that summer, when the sickness—a sickness of my language—was upon me and had gutted me so completely that without inhibition I could fill myself with true or untrue memories, I often thought that certain passages from that old pornography were still hiding in crannies of my brain, anticipating a chance to emerge into my consciousness. I was instantly suspicious of them; I couldn't even recall the words of the scrap of writing I'd thought I'd read through the rain-washed bus window six months before. I didn't think it possible that in my attempt to write an obscene text I'd been interested in anything more than cobbling together the torrid visions of my imagination; still less would I have aimed for social relevance. But in my attempts to conjure up the text, those sorts of associations kept intruding. Possibly I was already rehabilitating myself in my own eyes by inflating the text's value. But never, I told myself, will I hit on the real roots of my past aberration unless I stop cultivating the coarseness of my feelings, and I'll never find the seat of my language's sickness unless I utterly expose myself, for it seems clear that the schizophrenia of my language had already set in back then.

Yes, it was a sickness of my language…since early that year I'd been tracking its symptoms on long nighttime rambles, again and again I'd wandered down country roads, untrafficked at that hour, until I reached the edge of that great, lonely trash heap whose shadowy waste was riven by red restless fires, illuminated by a subterranean glow, populated by rats and sick stray dogs, a strangely magical destination for me…and a point of departure, I told myself. — I was no longer able to put a "normal" text on paper, a simple careless description, without strange, overwrought accusations getting mixed in, attempts to compensate for some revolting cowardice of my soul. Invariably it took just slight provocations—and invariably they were similar in nature—to summon a perfidious feeling within me, a kind of seething ferment that instantly propelled me from the place where I was sitting, made me jump up and rush out into the streets of the deserted nighttime town, and chased me from town at a hysterical pace, as though the blazing panic in my guts were visible from the few lit windows in the houses.

My outward body hastened utterly insensate through the night, while within me language was embedded in the musty, diffuse but tenacious miasma of an unfathomable old fear, captive words thrashing in nebulous webs that stretched denser and finer the more strands and loops were ruptured by the terrified movements. What were my words doing in that thicket's midst? I asked myself. Maybe they were trying to mate and couldn't pull it off: go away! Come back! Stay here!... They were words spoiled by mistrust of the place where they were spoken. — I seemed to recall that, similarly, I'd bedded the *I* of that early pornographic text within a substance much like a damp, decaying thicket. It was unclear to me whether I wasn't grafting my present lusts onto that early text, but I believed I'd described myself lying down with a girlfriend— whom I called *callous* and whose head was sometimes concealed from me entirely—on a soft bed of different kinds of hair, heaps of women's hair... tresses, thick braids, wild half-spoiled snarls offering protection from the icy cold of a filthy concrete floor; fear and loathing of this hair merged with the shamelessness of our lust. — Some childhood experience must have caused these imaginings; I had no recollection of it. In eternal, implacable hatred toward my childhood I had suppressed, among other things, the memory of that experience. It must have been connected to the empty barracks of the concentration camp on the edge of M., which was my chief playground until about the age of twelve, because the camp—bordering a vast expanse of rubble that had once been munitions factories, with scattered parts of buildings still standing that were now used to produce replacement parts for radios—was located very close to our house. At the time I felt I was the only child who knew the barracks' hellish purpose; I was the child whose imagination, when playing in the long bare rooms, would not let him picture the ugly brown spatters and spots on the whitewashed walls as anything other than blood, nor let him avoid envisioning corpses or groaning torture victims strung up on the rusty hooks in the masonry. And it's possible that the criminal imagination of the child I was, watching the others play hide-and-seek in the rubble and the barracks, coupled horror at the camp's former reality with my first childish desires. — I had heard or read that the prisoners' hair had been shorn, that even the women had been utterly stripped of their hair, and I thought up that story in which we bedded on mounds of hair, and even amid those mounds I imagined the smell of women's pubic hair, though I'd never even seen it before. My language was filled with hair, hair surged and swept in the flow of words I poured forth, in fall the ailing bare trees beyond the trash heaps wore wigs of hair and smoke, the dump trucks tossed it to the wind on the slopes of the defunct strip mines. Hair, whose presence I suspected in the trash cans on the wayside. Hair, to which I was relegated as a piece of human trash who refused to help collect the trash. With the hair-matted trash of his writing paper on a desk concealed from the world. With a brain damned beneath the storm-tossed wig, damned by the voice of my mother, by the voice of the state in the tone of my mother. Disapproval of my hair, which risked ending up in a camp. Ending in those barracks I knew from my childhood. Where hair blew through the window gaps in the evening, hair from the camps, hair from the ramp. And it seemed as if my entire surroundings, the entire country were changing into a place like the places where I played as a child. As if hair were being hoarded, forgotten, lost hair behind all the hills of this country. Hair that could not be saved unless I took it up into my language. Into my isolated, snarled language, sick with shameful smells, and flying yellow beneath the sky in the sickly color of King David. — From far off I see the barracks of my childhood, and know of nothing inside them but scatterings of rubble, long ice-cold rooms, white-washed and spattered, dully spattered with liquids turned black, whitewashed once again, why if not for some ominous reason, spattered once again,

pissed on, wildly scrawled on with lascivious rhom-
boids. Nothing in this cold place, but when evening
comes, when, playing in these rooms, the indefinable lustful mystery grows, brown, brunette, fox-red
darkness surges in long skeins through the frameless
window squares, billows in the corners, conceals
from the searchers those who are hiding, evening
hair that hid me, evening that smelled of urine and
whitewash, shadow-webs that caught me.
Shadow-hair that hid me when I gasped out the
shameful smells of my thoughts under the yellow
rain trickling from the moon, powerless in the sharp
shadow by the barrack window, powerless against
the lust of the sickness that revolved inside my head,
powerless against the world to which I couldn't reveal my lust, which knew it all the same, for all my
latecomings and shortcomings were the result of my
banishment into unauthorized desire. And the
nights came with hair whose sheen had grown dull,
damp and moldy, hair that no longer burned. On
top were remnants swept together from the ramp,
mixed with boot-mud that had turned to dust with
the years. — And when I returned to town one

summer night in a year when no rain fell, I dug my arm into one of the trash cans. And I thought I felt hair, a fleshy hairy mound in the midst of the can whose contents massed around my wrist. Just as though I've managed to swallow my own fist, a labial circle closes, firm and sucking, around my lower arm, bent arm wrapped around the neck of my shadow, pressing the head of my shadow to my face, gingerly I've closed the fingers of the hand on that arm to form a fist, and for days to come, on the palm of my hand and between my fingers, I'll find the smell of the heat that my fist clutched. Rotten fruit in the trash can, rotten glowing fruit and its wet heat, sinking into the fingers' skin, into the clefts of the four-fingered surface of the fist, smoothly coating it with a juice from those depths. My language smoothly coated with the color of this sickness. The yellow color of a wall before my language. The yellow-gray color of a door no key now fits. My speech closing when I say: My fist is stuck in flesh. Returning when I say: In gently swollen flesh, in a hole beneath the hair. Returning to the maw of origin, ball of the hand, held by brain-like stems and windings, bathed by my slit veins, held fast in the center of the flood and wound in the vortex of the brain, rotten fruit in the trash can. — In that instant I knew the speech I had to deliver, that I should have delivered back in winter at the labor office, that I'd have to deliver in court before summer's end. It was the instant when my hand in the trash can met resistance, a round soft object resembling a uterus, and I started, scalded by fright, for suddenly here was something that I was forbidden to harm. — Someone had scribbled *Jackie I love you* on the wall of a nearby house, and every night I stood and gazed at those words, consumed by envy; they never faded, because it never rained that summer. Head blazing, I swayed in the night's heat and dug my nails into the heels of my hands: an awful venereal disease raged in the windings of my brain while my arm, in the quivering profusion of this trash can, was paralyzed in boneless fear. All at once I'd lost my name, which I'd need to begin the speech with. A ferment and blaze in the skull, the silent emanation of my paralysis, the inert rotten substance of the sun on a woman's neck, and my name burning under her wig.

This name that sundered me from everything a man was. But I knew I had to change into a man, into a name. What wall of reasons had severed me from that Something called *Jack*, *Caesar*, *Dante*, and severed me from those three words on the wall? What mountain of pedagogy, from which I'd rolled down, yet still could not share in love's banal mystery? Oh, what tumor of reasons, blocking me from even a tainted surrogate for love? All that was left to me of love, a grimy scrap of pornography, had ended up in the trash heap, and only there, on those soggy notes that had so repelled my mother, could my true name still be found; my humid head held it no longer. It was the name I needed for my signature, to identify myself with the speech I had to deliver at the labor office. The speech I meant to give as an introduction to those three famous words. The three words, spun, sprung from that gaping head that would rear up on its stem, having at last hatched those three twitching eggs in its summer brain. Those three shrill words, to discharge them at last into the tresses of that Leading Functionary behind the yellow doors of that bureaucratic labyrinth. To fling at last those three yolk-words, those three hoarse ejaculations across the desk, across the judge's bench, to hurl them at last into the midst of the statistical papers, into the orderliness of those indices, at last to bedew the files' pernicious pornography with my *I*. — No, it was useless; I lacked a name; I'd have to deliver my speech in the name of the general public. And so my speech might need to be delivered with my fist.

No, each night the three words I'd invented were answered only by a cripple. — There was nothing in that trash can to interest me. Nothing to love—truly, the contents of that cylinder precisely matched those of the cornucopia left for me by the Republic for the purpose of my education. None of those contents could be unambiguously named. — It wasn't long before I felt wretched again. In just five minutes I concluded I lacked the education to *glimpse* the females, even if they were still present, even if they existed by the millions. To see them it was too little to be blind in one eye, it was too little that I had some anatomical notion of them from the time my mother let me visit the circus as a child. — Already Lenin, as recorded by Clara Zetkin, had described *wallowing in sexuality* as a *hobby of the intellectuals* for which there was no place in the *class-conscious* proletariat; the adjective denoted a level of consciousness miles above my own. Resignedly, I turned away from the trash can and regarded my arm, still damp past the wrist; I looked at my fist, which opened helplessly, harmless and hopeless, as though there'd never be any place for it either

And yet there had been something...I was already walking away, but now I retraced my steps... hadn't I discovered a beautiful object in the trash can, yes, it seemed to me that inside the trash can yesterday I'd felt a kind of uterus. I lowered my hand in once more, seized a round, firm object that had a certain weight and that I could pull effortlessly from the jumble of hair, filth, wet substances, old clothes. I couldn't see what I'd brought to light, for there were no lights on this dark street...or I saw only what I wanted to see. Even so, I thought I'd found something unmistakably female. But what? I cursed the town's dysfunctional lighting, even Lady Luna dimmed her radiance as though to follow her lovely playmates. — What should I do? I was free,

free and nameless; but, divested of reality, I could not do a thing.

If I was free, then I was free from reality—*free*, I felt the impact of the word sink in; the light I had seen was the flash of a stinging ideological slap in the face. — As of this morning I was free: let go from the factory, that is. The only outcome of this thought was that time collapsed back into its proper dimensions: early that morning, after a bitter altercation in which I'd threatened to thrash my boss, I'd been fired; right afterward I'd taken the bus to A. to complain about it at the labor office, and that evening I'd returned from A. Many things might have happened in that time, but my hours had filled up with repetitions and absurdities, absurd attempts at the speech I'd kept making all day, until ultimately I'd spoken in exactly the wrong place—assuming that wasn't just a figment of my imagination—and I'd probably said exactly the wrong things. Oh, in that wrong place…which, naturally, was the right place for my destructivity…I might have slandered the females, might have chased them away, and now I finally had to face up to my idiocies. It was probably the very gaffes and idiocies of what I said that could be directly linked to my identity, my name, but my idiocies by themselves could hardly meet with sympathy in our republic's bureaucracies. — I hereby request permission—I believed I'd started off—I request permission, effective immediately, to wear skirts, even outside the home, without facing a reprimand for indecent behavior. — I pondered whether I'd really spoken those words; the one single bottle clutched in my fist couldn't have been enough to make me do it. — And without, say, being subjected to that famous reflexological Pavlovian therapy: I'm not a homosexual. Please make a note of that. And I'm not just trying to blasphemously shock a fatherland that has evidently had all of its female parts castrated, I'm trying to make sure that, following my dismissal from the factory, the only one I'd consider setting foot in, I won't be carted off to a labor camp for antisocial behavior if the factory can't hire me back. So it's not just fetishistic foolishness that's made me start collecting women's clothing from the trash; I'm trying to finally dismiss the state security forces from my trouser's fly, where their employees made themselves at home early on, I'm trying to finally give them their freedom. Somewhere out there in town are three words that must be ancient, written on a public wall where everyone can read them, addressed to *Jack the Ripper*, to whom in many ways I could probably be compared—or at least I belong, albeit by a strange coincidence, to a nationality of similar characters—thus those three words, in some tricky way, must also be addressed to me, or must have been at one time, and I'm anxious to assert my claim to that avowal on the wall without the labor office hindering me with terms and demands. Don't ask me just who I think I am; I'm not fond of these kinds of polemics myself. But now that I lack the money to buy a ticket, I have to put on my own cabaret…oh, and I did so love the ladies' revue. At least my idiocies, at this moment, help me realize that I have a right to those three words. —

Of course—I was pacing back and forth among the trash cans, seemingly sedate, but clenching my fists in disappointment—of course I hadn't begun with any such tirade, it was too idiotic, it wasn't in keeping with my striving toward higher things…

had I even started speaking at all? In A. I'd fallen victim to the usual blind alleys between the institutions. It was outside the labor office's business hours, but an older man who was locking the door behind him asked me what I wanted. It was utterly superfluous, he said, to ask about a job at the labor office, because every enterprise in the country was looking for people. The notices hung on every factory gate, visible from afar. For untrained workers there was still the trash collection service, though in summer it was idle and thus they were choosy about new employees. Had I had that sort of trouble there? After all, I wasn't dealing with the capitalist world here...he added slyly, and coming all this way had been, at the very least, futile. — I then walked across the entire town to the labor court to ask for an appointment with the public prosecutor, but she wasn't there, even though her office hours had already begun. — Would I prefer to speak to her secretary or wait an hour until she arrived? — I decided to wait, but when I asked an hour later, I was turned away again with the same words. Once more I spent a full hour wandering the town aimlessly,

losing confidence in all my neatly prepared rhe-
torical statements. On my punctual return to the
courthouse an hour later—now I was addressed by a
higher-ranking bureaucrat who had joined the policemen at the front desk—I was told that it was
much too late to consult with the public prosecutor, the office hours had ended long ago. It would
be pointless to come back for at least another week,
and besides it was safer to apply in writing. — The
situation seemed so typical of my entire life up to
that point, seemed so perfectly to describe my relationship to this country's society, that I almost felt a
flush of gratitude. But that was only after my protest
gave way to a kind of epiphany: Of course, in some
confounded fashion, it was always I who brought
myself to this point, even though I wasn't quite sure
how I'd pulled it off this time. At least it gave me a
considerable reprieve before having to offer an explanation. And indeed it was impossible to do anything but come too late, however hard you tried. It
was impossible to be released *in time* from captivity.
— Thoughts racing, I searched the town center for a
pub, but there was no room in the two or three bars

I found; only at the station bar, filled with hollering men, did I manage to quench my thirst for beer. I drank sour, stale beer, and already I'd missed the first bus to M., so I went on drinking. Soon I was asking myself what I'd wanted in A. anyway—why the labor court, of all places? What had I planned to tell the prosecutor to avoid being told that they'd been quite right to fire me? Your attitude toward work is well known to us, Herr C.; for your own sake, you ought to look for a new job immediately... Anyway, the place where you've been barred from employment is mainly a women's factory. — How could they muster any sympathy for me when I put forth my arguments without paranoia, citing perfectly objective things such as age and illness? In this republic, sick language is simply a necessity of life, it's the only means possible, I thought with relief. — Have yourself examined, they'd surely have advised me— yet it was I who had to examine myself. Here in this republic, though, I had no possibility whatsoever of doing so.

Whenever I'd felt within me the unforeseen power to examine myself, even to know myself, and consequently, perhaps, expunge the germs of my sickness, I found that the state snatched every tool from my hands, or hid all those tools from me, obscuring the means of ascertaining any kind of probability. The inevitable result was a serious disease, a pervasive disease of my ability to really and truly perceive the world, and a disease of my ability to truly make myself known to another person as a figure in reality. For me, reality had been stolen and annihilated, so by necessity I had to exist as a form of annihilated reality, as a mere *delusion of reality*, and by that same token had to annihilate the reality of the people around me.

What, for instance, could the labor court possibly care when I lamented my fear of impotence? What an incredibly sad, pathetic question. Was that why they hadn't let me in? There being no injustice in this country, there could be no justice either…I sensed that this sort of mental short circuit was already part of my speech. And—now the scales fell from my eyes—what I should have demanded from the bureaucrats was some kind of archive collecting complaints about *the psychological transgressions of the past against the present*; such a bureau, I now realized, was the only thing that could vindicate the existence of this country's justice system. But there was no such bureau, or else that too had been kept secret from me. Desperately I wondered to whom I could turn. — There was no doubt in my mind that the person heading such an institution would have to be a woman, by no means a man; that, for me, was in the very nature of things…but when I tried to prove it, I was at a loss; once again I felt I would need almost visionary abilities to perceive the most natural, self-explanatory, and necessary things. I had to *hallucinate* in order to discover the world and the possibilities I had for living in it. But if I lacked the strength for that, even in a brief spell of faintness, those possibilities vanished, seemed to vanish forever, everything I could love vanished, justice vanished, right and wrong vanished, my hopes and reproaches vanished…everything I loved to touch vanished, happiness vanished, the women vanished. — Indeed, I probably vanished myself. I looked around in the station bar, and saw nothing but men, drunken, palavering, wildly gesticulating men who seemed to be talking away furiously at invisible opponents; I'd been noticed as little as if I'd never come in. And yet it soon seemed to me that accusations loomed from the stifling air, accusations about the isolation in which I sat, the isolation that was dissolving me. — I can't be held responsible for the mistakes of this male society, I argued in my defense: not I alone. There are certain limitations I couldn't possibly transcend. I've come too late, even on the occasions when those mistakes I'm referring to were made, Chairwoman. — You were dismissed too late, you mean. — For heaven's sake, I cried, I've come to reverse my dismissal. — You'll have to explain in full; you'll have to pull yourself together and explain everything in full from the very beginning. Pull yourself together, remember what it means to you to get your job back. — Actually it means nothing, I replied, actually all it means, Madam Counsel, is that it was there, in that factory, that I was first able to recollect all the things that ultimately precipitated my dismissal. I think they go back to when I was about your daughters' age, Madam Chairwoman, yes, maybe that's when it began. At some point back then I underwent an amputation. Metaphorical, of course, not literal. No diseased limb was removed, but it was an amputation all the same, a mental amputation, a lobotomy. In the splendid springtime of my life, I suddenly caught a chill…since then the days have sped past. Believe me, now, compared to your daughters, my nature is that of someone twice as old. But recently I seemed to have been rejuvenated, evidently blossoming. No longer in my first youth, but still fairly healthy, I'm telling you, at least to a certain extent I imagined I was. Healthy, then, and with my life laid out before me; I had work, yes I did, I worked up until this summer. Of course I'd rather have been writing…you know I tried my hand at that, but I was working in a so-called women's factory, day after day I went with the greatest of pleasure to work directly under the women. And as I did I recalled my youth; my youth was a kind of metastasis that grew out of me, not always to my advantage, but youth all the same…but now that factory has been amputated from me, just one more cruel intervention in my fate. And perhaps that completed my amputations. All at once I lost more cells, cells that steered me…perhaps they steered my breath, the crooks of my knees, my vocal cords, perhaps they steered the voice I put to paper, albeit unsuccessfully. Perhaps amputation is the wrong word, and I should speak of castration, castration that mutilated my interior world. I wasn't operated on, it was all left attached to me, but the cells that steered it were dimmed; my cells, certain cells of mine, were sterilized and castrated. It was a castration of the brain, and fair femininity was the forceps they used.

It's hard for me to describe the methods they employed, and it embarrasses me, *Madam Magister*. The whole affair…both my explanations and the conclusions I draw from them…is embarrassing, ludicrous, anything but *manly*, the way I ought to be. And death is near. Oh, I find these things obscene, but I must try to explain them. I *must*, I say. And my hope is that the method, if it was one, will seem less obscene to you than the tone of my explanation. In other words, the obscene thing is not *what* I'm explaining, the obscene thing is *how* I explain it…I'm telling you this, *Madam Magister*, in order to stay in your good graces…so in many ways the manner of my account is identical with its moral. *Moral*, admittedly, is a rather old-fashioned word, not very popular nowadays…at most one speaks of the *morale* of soldiers or workers…but the latest version of the word, the sense in which I'm using it, goes back to the period I'm starting in; even then the word was the flag under which I was castrated. I grew up within walls that resounded with the din of this word's two vowels, within walls where, as in any ordinary madhouse, my prick was regarded as dangerous. As you know, the mission of psychopathology is to kill all natural urges. I grew up under the rule of psychopathologists who declared the sex drive to be abnormal…and *sex* to be capitalistic; the very word was practically banned for sounding too American. I'm not exaggerating, the documents are still available, and you know all this yourself anyway, you're only a little bit younger than I am, you're about as old as my mother, and no doubt you collaborated on those sorts of communiqués back then… in short, even then science was holding a shielding hand over me. They had a dim premonition of the calamity arising from the pricks of my generation; they didn't have enough money back then to buy up the young people's sexual interests; the state threatened to collapse if they couldn't keep the pricks down. Perhaps they could have explained this to me in scientific terms, but even then, it seems, there was only limited access to the academic departments that kept the sexological ledgers. Though I belonged to the class for whom the products of Enlightenment thought were intended, they were not revealed to us in their pure form; instead, they were instantly translated into action. And so—it was a very enlightened method—they began to sever me from the consciousness of my prick, the Enlightenment took charge of that consciousness itself, for the cleanliness of my feelings had to be preserved. Oh, they compared me to a starfish, and lectured me in its reproductive methods. In fact, the word *clean* usually played the chief role in speaking of interpersonal relationships; the term seemed obligatory in that context. That gave me pause, for I knew that my prick pissed and dangled near my anus, *Madam Magister.* — It was *smut*—I'm inserting a little anecdote so you don't get bored—it was filthy smut, I learned during my first police interrogation, which happened in sixth—I think, unless it was earlier—sixth grade, after they'd confiscated some female nudes from us in the schoolyard—where are the rest of the naked ladies, a police officer bellowed at me, frightening me out of my wits—nudes drawn in exercise books, drawn in a manner that did not obfuscate the existence of genitalia. Incidentally it wasn't me, I have to say in my defense; I was arrested merely for sneering at the drawings' poor quality, which probably raised suspicions that I dabbled in that kind of artwork myself. That wasn't the case, but I have to admit that the little drawings had lodged so firmly in my mind that four or five years later I myself became a pornographer...and probably to this day I can't *see* the females because there's nothing to be found anywhere that compares with those pictures...I became a pornographer myself, albeit in prose, effusions that probably all landed in the trash, which is why it's no blasphemy if the depths of a trash can remind me of a gaping pelvis. My home was duly searched, but nothing was found;

he's probably hid that smut where no one can find it, was the conclusion the officers conveyed to my teachers, who stood frozen in attitudes of revulsion. Thus nothing, not even my innocence, was proven, all that was proven was the necessity of making a note for the files branding me as a highly problematic prospect for any kind of higher education. Thus, *Madam Magister*, academia remained closed to me, and I became a worker; I desire to remain one, in a factory of my choice, and that is the reason for my speech.

But I'm not finished yet, *Madam Magister.* I shall proceed with increasingly obscene expositions. Even then, you see, it was clear that the country would have to be divided, the ends of this undertaking were sacred, and required means that had little to do with reform. — I must have been crazy even back then, perhaps even crazier than now; I suddenly imagined the country's partition first being performed through the waists of the females, so delicately that they'd never even notice…the females' lower bodies, their perfumed refinement—or so I gathered from the polemical stew my brain was fed—belonged on the other side of the wall in the reactionary camp, where they'd be stuffed with money. Naturally that had to repel me. Some of the lower bodies did in fact stay here, allocated to the academics studying how the situation would develop—specifically, those lower bodies whose prospects for education were less problematic than mine, and which, at that time, seemed to comprise more female lower bodies than male. To my alarm I realized that my prick—which had been provoking me for some time—aimed over this wall, that is, at the females' lower bodies, but my head still wished to remain here... Oh, I realized that the females' upper bodies also remained here as well, buttoned-up torsos dressed in gray or blue, with muscular arms longing to embrace the rebuilding of the country— that's a quote, though I wish I'd forgotten both the quote and the source. And the heads of the females remained here as well, heads filled with clean thoughts, heads that would reward me with brotherly love if I managed to do my part to rebuild. But a leaden prick dangled in front of my accomplishments...the ache in this tiny organ was leaden...

and whenever I began to feel some obscene pride in it, I learned that this pride by no means resonated with the females. You see, from the literature that wasn't prohibited, that I was allowed to trust, I thought I'd learned that in fact the females detested my prick—once again I'm simplifying things rather crudely, *Madam Magister*, I was an uninvited guest in the literary sphere, and the literature I was permitted to read was one that couldn't corrupt me— and, avid to learn something about the relationship between my prick and the females, I felt great respect for everything available in print. From all I was able to learn about the problem, it seemed conclusive that my prick was distasteful to the females; the females, I believed, preferred to go to bed with Enlightenment literature; I was at best a sad case study in those disquisitions. This threw me into a panic, but I received words of comfort…I should wait and see, stay calm, for heaven's sake give myself time, I was told, by the newspapers, that is, for I had no confidante; yes, the newspapers were beginning now and then, in the section aimed at young people, to touch on questions of the relations between the sexes…stay calm, and it was as though I were being handed a bar of soap for my prick, because, I was told, the hearts of my future partners were clean. Indeed, I knew that in their hearts the females loved men such as Lenin, who had no prick…or at least nothing was known about Lenin's prick. Oh, I took the bar of soap and I washed my prick; out of sheer sympathy with the females I'd begun to detest my prick just as much as they did. And at last I was fit, fit for life, fit for military service, but to my surprise the females were still only to be found in other institutions. And when at last I was allowed to behold them, from an appropriate distance, I assented to their coldness. Everything was perfectly simple; for sheer love of the females and assisted by their image—knit stockings and the blue shirts of the Socialist Youth—I castrated myself, and no one but I was the surgeon. — What a joke, Madam, what a sordid joke, though not much more sordid than the one being played on me now, in what's jocularly called my second youth…my second, for now everything is repeating for me. Mediocrely…everything repeats mediocrely now, with a mediocre smell. While I, with mediocre success, feel relegated to the lowest category, feel I've found my place; while I, with mediocre success, have forgotten all that tormented me, with modest savings to supplement the pension I'll soon receive, looking back at my mediocre success on the firing ranges of our national defense...at least I seemed motivated by the declared aim of protecting women and children, an aim for which I was found halfway fit...meanwhile, I've suddenly been severed from the females again. And I no longer see the females, Madam, my sight has been dimmed by some awful delusion... once again they're only to be found in other institutions. — But now the academics have cleared the decks, torn off the superfluous buttons, now the breasts can emerge from those blue shirts. Incredible but true, at least that's my impression...and I'd gone completely unaware of it. There's a phrase of Frantz Fanon's that describes an ugly emotion, a precursor to violence; for Fanon it's revolutionary violence: *lustful envy*. That's it, Madam: that describes exactly what I feel when I realize how many things I've been oblivious to. Suddenly the academics are acknowledging the lower body, grinning as they announce the results of their experiments. Suddenly they pat us on the shoulders, shaking their heads...claiming not to understand what we've been doing with our lives...didn't we know, hadn't we heard that sexuality is crucial to personal development? The academics have known that for years, and tested it out most productively—and they present us with excerpts from relevant literature purchased on their trips abroad. Good Lord, in their articles they call it sex now themselves. And they can't understand how we could have gone without it, they don't understand how dried up we are, dried up to the point of desperation, oh, the hell with it, they just turn to embrace a new generation. The question is what do we want now, with our dried-up fingers?... What are we complaining about, anyway, they introduced public abortion, they talked about two timing...theoretically possible even for you, Mr. Oldtimer... The academics can point to certain successes: the introduction of the bathtub, the Orgasm Organization, the Party orgy... the introduction of the masquerade, the introduction of the nipple, the importation of *four-letter words*. I haven't been doing too badly, either, I became the proud owner of a television set, I could gaze at my reflection in the tube that had digested my youth. — With my slightly obscene sense of humor, with slight regret, I proceed to surmise that people have grown a bit weary of all these academic goings-on. Perhaps I should envy them even this weariness, I don't know. I stand by at a loss, my brain a blank, *Madam Magister*, I don't even understand the foreign expressions. I'm forced to realize that all the things that nearly killed me are utterly irrelevant for nearly everyone else. — But I set out, I raced around the country…I scrambled for jobs…I hurried across construction sites just to track down the females, time after time I swore to ignore my impotence. In the end, at last, I thought I'd come close to the females once more, I found a suitable factory, every day I was allowed to be under them, often with nothing but a metal grate between us; but now I've been fired from my women's factory, once again the sight of the females has been castrated from my skull, and that's what I wanted to complain about,

Madam Chairwoman. — Now you'll tell me I'm exaggerating, operating with generalizations…but you're the one who performed the operation. You'll say I've made a fool of myself, I proved my own inadequacy, I myself am to blame for everything…but still you want to hear the conclusions I've come to. — I know just one conclusion, there's just one that comes to mind, and that is. *j'accuse.* Away with them, that's the conclusion, I never want to see them again…you neither, Madam Prosecutor. You're no female, Madam Prosecutor, you're my father. And my mother raves about you to this day, just because you screwed her once. You won't bestow your love on me anyway, I'm not good enough for you, you told me that over and over. And there's only one conclusion: I protest. Yes, I protest… Leaping up from the table, I yelled that last sentence out into the station bar. My voice was so hysterical that I flinched at it myself; I glanced around, shamefaced. The beer-guzzling men hadn't taken the slightest notice of me; completely self-absorbed, they hadn't even raised their heads. I tossed a few coins onto the table, more than covering my bill, and left the bar in a hurry.

Of course, I thought, there's a peculiar paradox inherent in my account. For, though it's a fact that I chased the women all over this country, and from all the bars where I've lurked I've been incapable of staring in any direction but theirs, in some way I've always avoided them, too. Yes, I knew they enjoyed the love of a state that ordered me to look them cleanly in the face. The state that ordered me to do this must have seen me as essentially filthy. Filth… from the very beginning I must have been filth to them, just a filthy, greasy worker's uniform. But I have to say, I avoided the women out of cleanliness, out of cleanliness I avoided them like a leper… like a leper. Now I understand that the cleanliness commended to me was leprosy, evil-smelling, snot-green–oozing leprosy. — Again I looked at my hands, where some indefinable foamy substance seemed to have dried into a dark scab reaching up my lower arms…is this some sickness I've caught from the trash can? I asked myself. — What cleanliness underneath, I thought, what cleanliness under this peeling, where my skin is in continual rosy renewal. It's just the kind of sight that would drive away the women, in the face of this cleanliness they've made themselves invisible, and the source of the cleanliness is my brow, the castration scabs on my brow that constantly spread like wildfire over my skin.

I was coming from the trash heaps, heading down into town; the bus from A. drove past me, and I saw the men sitting in its brightly lit interior on the way to their night shift in the factories of M....for a moment I thought I saw women sitting in the bus, even my mother coming back from a trip, but I must have been mistaken. — An awful loneliness came over me; at that moment I would have given everything, half my life, to be able to sit on the bus among those workers...I'd even have given up my attempts at writing had that been the condition for being hired back. My writing attempts, which the women found so alarming...only on very rare, exceptional occasions had I'd dared confess to a woman that I was trying my hand at literature, but my brow bore the stigma of this contemptible secret. — I recalled that once, at the age of six or seven, I'd confessed to my mother in a fit of blind faith that I wanted to be a writer, in fact that I'd already begun and was writing constantly, and my most fervent desire was to be allowed, one day, to read my efforts to her. My mother, though barely replying to this disclosure, showed every sign of being rudely surprised. First skeptical whether to believe my fraudulent words, and expressing indignation at them, her face turned into a mask of such violent suspicion that I fell silent at once, then resorted to calming her down. Presumably it was just my childish impression I was recalling; in reality, perhaps, my mother was incapable of taking me that seriously… but I thought I saw her tremble, only her bewilderment preventing her from instantly recognizing me as a wretched traitor to all her intentions for me; I began to placate her, saying that I'd pursue such things only to pass the time, of course, I'd write only in hours that I truly had to spare, and never would any of my stories describe the true circumstances of our life. Though my mother seemed relieved, her face remained mistrustful, her initial pallor giving way to a blush of shame, as though, without guessing it myself, I'd just voiced a crass obscenity in front of her or announced my intention to betray every utterance made in our home to the neighbors, the public, the secret police. I hastened to assure her that my writing attempts would not compromise my obligations in the slightest; they would not worsen my performance at school any further, or conflict with society's moral demands upon me, nor would they induce me to abandon even one of the ideals, ideological or hygienic, impressed upon me by the home, the school, and the world. In particular, I'd always respect my family life; she could rest assured of that: the public, should I ever enjoy its attention, would learn nothing to our disadvantage. — Wasn't I ashamed of myself, she finally asked, to be thinking about a public at all, what with all the nonsense I had in my head? But fortunately I'd never even make it that far, fortunately that wasn't even possible for a person from such a humble background. You needed a special gift for that, or at least the wherewithal to hold your own in select circles. — But I have that gift, I retorted. — What kind of a gift? she asked. Your father was a person with a talent for everything. Everyone knew him as an excellent

tailor, and he sacrificed himself entirely for his profession and his family. He was a paragon of pro-
priety and goodness, welcome everywhere and liked
by everyone. He was someone people could rely on,
but you've turned out just the opposite. One would
think that you weren't his son at all, that you'd turn
out to be nothing but an unskilled laborer, cleaning
up after other people. You'll probably just end up on
the wrong track, and all your life you'll do nothing
but disgrace us. — And so, I thought, I've actually
lived up to her opinion of me.

That bus, barreling past the trash heaps without
stopping—I should have flagged it at the bus stop,
or, even better, hurled myself down onto the road,
right in front of the snout of that bellowing beast
carrying life away in its belly, I should have let myself be run over rather than hold back—wasn't that
bus a constant menace to me…hadn't it once given
me a ride after all, picked me up from the side of
the road? I tried frantically to remember when that
could have been. All I could recall was the scene
itself, filled with such deathly dread that I could
never board the bus with an easy mind again: it had

been packed, but no one had taken the seat beside me, in the aisle behind me the women remained standing, and from that day on I seemed shut out of life. I felt I was in a tightly locked case, being flown through a space where all my memory was annihilated, and from that moment on I knew I was in hell, every single fiber of my being. I arrived in town that evening not knowing how I'd gotten there, August, the month of my birth, or at least I hoped time could still be defined so precisely. The air was brown that evening…by that time of day I'd already been born, a little bundle, appalled to the point of stupefaction, lying paralyzed in its cage and staring out at its first night…the brown seemed to be sucked up by a black yawn, and somewhere in that blackout sparks glowed, eerily red, giving no light, emitting nothing but smoke, heavy noxious smoke. — The town received me with great silence—the spellbound silence that anticipates an attack—and with an emptiness whose borders seemed sealed, so that even now I found myself inside an empty container…and I was part of the emptiness, I was its empty, reinstated consciousness. I had misgivings about returning to my apartment…I could make no headway against my aimlessness; I had grasped that life was a crude, clumsy fake.

A while later, standing in front of the police station, I began to shout—that much I could remember—I shouted something several times, as loudly as I could. I waited for a reaction, perhaps for someone to recognize me and arrest me…I felt that after the speech I'd trumpeted in A.—loud and hopefully clear for all to hear—I ought to have been locked up at once…but no reaction came, or if so, only a stupid, empty-headed reaction: grins at how long it had taken me to realize that everything…the whole republic, the whole world…had been faked.

I dreaded the apartment…at least the part of it I'd barricaded myself in…for some time now its dark, unclean chaos had filled me with indefinable horror. For a long while I'd been at loggerheads with my mother—who occupied the other, larger part of the apartment—as, like some inexorable toxic swamp, my disorder, my filth had begun encroaching on her space. Now that my mother was gone—as a retiree, she was allowed to go abroad, and she'd been staying with her sister in West Germany for more than a month now—this swamp had overwhelmed her part of the apartment. The dark stench lingered in her rooms as well, because I never opened the windows, because moldy stacks of unwashed dishes towered on the windowsills, because even here I smoked without stopping, though my mother always protested vehemently. Until recently my body had seemed to cope effortlessly with an insane degree of chain-smoking, so I'd gotten into the habit of letting the butts burn in the overflowing ashtrays... or rather I lined up the old butts with the embers of the ones I'd just discarded, so that gradually all the butts ignited and burned all the way through, until—meanwhile I was smoking a new cigarette—crackling, blue-black clouds rose and settled on the ceiling, concealing it behind a flood of smoke three feet deep or more. More and more I was falling prey to fears—as I planted my elbows in the litter on the desktop, capable only of smoking without cease, as I let the desk lamp burn on—increasingly menacing fears of the movements I thought I glimpsed overhead, which I was trying to cloak with smoke clouds…but now the movements went on behind the smoke and their obscurity increased my fear.

Fear made me switch off the desk lamp and light a candle…though sitting by candlelight made me uneasy, a constant reminder of the air raids, when we were nearly always left without power. A vile, sneaky movement below the ceiling seemed to roil the swathes of smoke, and I moved nervously to the kitchen, sweeping ancient bundles of newspapers from the blue-and-white checked oilcloth that covered the table, noisome, nauseating, spittle-covered newspapers, stuck together and rendered illegible by the liquor from tomatoes rotted to black…I always bought lots of tomatoes, those so-called love apples, which I devoured with great pleasure on good days; but now they'd all gone sour on me, gone soft, gone bad…and from their detritus too-dark vapors seemed to rise. There were noises on the street as though shots were being fired…at the same time I felt that a sluggish unrest had erupted in the lurking night outside the window, that down there the weary tread of many feet was shuffling, stumbling in one common direction. — There's nothing behind the smoke on the ceiling, nothing, I said to myself. Nothing, just that cripple with cancer upstairs, whose mortal fear had made him move into the garret room, sitting up there, unyielding on his chair, day and night, staring over the roofs that ring the yard at the open country from where idiocy is closing in on him; the man whose old mother, with a wooden leg, tirelessly washed and fed him in years past, but now all the females have vanished from town. — Nothing, I said, and rested my cheek on the soothingly cool oilcloth covering the table, where the skin of my face immediately stuck to the tacky scab of liquid residues. At that moment I knew that this, and this alone, was the reason for my fear, the only solid reason: the nothingness, the void caused my eerie feeling, and against nothingness I was impotent.

The nothingness that frightened me was that I did nothing, nothing but breathe the horror of the night. I didn't even move as I breathed. Once, a week ago, two weeks, a letter had come, evidently for me and evidently from my mother, but I hadn't dared to open it; it was buried somewhere beneath the trash I'd piled up in the apartment. Now, all at once, I was tormented by the fear that the letter had been to announce her return...that suddenly, any moment now, the door might open and my mother might come in. She'd start shouting, throwing up her hands, without even an empty chair to collapse on. — I didn't have time, I was writing...so, shouting too, I'd attempt to explain the chaos. It would have been a lie, cruel self-mockery; for I'd written nothing, but once again I'd blame my writing for every evil that arose around me, I'd blame the sickness of my language, which would confirm my mother's position. Though she wouldn't even ask for proof of my claim; she never wasted a word on the subject, even when I was writing she condemned my *pastime* to scorn, and she was right to condemn me, for my writing was achieved at the price of filth and disorder, while I smoked and drank vast amounts of coffee. — You'll destroy yourself, she said, soon enough you'll see where this gets you, you'll destroy yourself and the lives of the people around you. — But she never told me what to live for...I was past forty, and so far she'd kept that a secret from me...

though she'd gone to the trouble to lug the madly
shrieking bundle that I was in the last years of the
war through the howling racket of the nighttime
air raids, dragging me down into the bomb shelter;
no, she hadn't just tossed me by the wayside, though
no one would ever have noticed. — Ah, and the
state hadn't tossed me away either…though it also
failed to explain what to live for, if not just to serve
it and increase the population it owned; to the state
it seemed obvious that I owed it boundless, eternal
gratitude. For ultimately it had created me…oh,
there'd been a progenetive act of incredible intensity: outstretched in sincerest devotion my mother
had let Father State bestride her in all the vigor of
his beauty; the grandiose symbol of rebuilding rose
precipitously before her and plunged into her body,
and to celebrate how she'd been favored, a sea of
flags unfurled, the Party's young guards waved them
over the rite of this clean coitus; I was immaculately
conceived and stood spotless amid the life that was
being rebuilt, my brow was steeled, I appeared in the
shape of hope…but then that one summer inflamed
this brow. Oh, only later did I dare to be jealous of

that pure act. Generalissimo Stalin, the friend of all good people, had created me; I had the honor of owing my life to him; I obeyed, and there was a weeping in the world, and tears on my mother's face as he departed from us. And I was scared to death...but desolate blazing summers inflamed me, and sweat flowed from my eyes. I closed my eyes, I must have fallen asleep...and woke up again in a terrible unbelief.

Waking up so late was one more cause for panic. — That night, after long sleepless rambles through the stifling apartment, back and forth between my room and the kitchen, after several failed attempts to fall asleep in my sweaty bed, I was revisited by a dream I'd dreamed often and with little variation. This time the dream was not interrupted by a signal rapped out above the room's ceiling, this time I dreamed the dream to its disturbing end, when its scenes, drained of color, faded into diffusion, into an unformed void where I was lost in indescribable fear. — This dream, which afflicted me only on nights when my mother was gone and I was defenseless, had always fled, leaving no memory, when the crutch of the cripple in the room above jabbed at the floorboards, imperiously demanding my silence; it seemed to disturb him when I cried out in my sleep, it scared him up from the immobility that made him one with the night's dull pulse that ebbed in the first hour of the new day, presaging his approaching death. Upon waking, all I ever knew was that I'd dreamed the words *I love you* or *Madam, I love you*, but I wasn't sure whether I'd cried the words out loud, as my cries had never startled me from sleep. — I knew that if the cripple still had any feelings for the things that were lost, these words had to drive him mad; yet for some time now I'd felt far more certain of hell than he.

One time I'd meant to go up and discuss that future in hell with him. — Probably I was mistaken even about that; it hadn't happened, I'd merely dreamed that intention too. Now, evidently, it was too late to act on it—I was horrified by the thought that that had nearly provoked me to go upstairs to the cripple to assail him with my envy, which might have been fatal for him. I'd escaped that fate, because now, presumably, he was dead. He'd gone and died when all the females left town...never again could I slink upstairs and listen at the door of his garret room to hear the halting dribble of his urine in a tin pot, the coughing when his mother lit his cigarette and he greedily sucked in the first drafts of smoke, the curses with which she admonished him for his impatience. — Now it was quiet up there, nothing to be heard but the summer's hum and crackle; amid the soft mass of yellow heat his gray face, with the bared teeth and the tip of his bitten tongue stuck between them—that mask that even in death seemed blinded by the sunbeam from the roof hatch—would slowly dry up. No, he wasn't in hell; even in the second when his heart finally stopped he'd had to fend off the sun, it wasn't in the night that his half-closed eyes grew dim, and what he saw wasn't the infernal plains of insurmountable garbage dumps with their flickering blood-red fires from which black locust swarms of charred paper whirled up, wasn't those hills and valleys of ash where a madman stumbled through the trash in search of a few long-rotted pages containing, in green ink, a few indecipherable instructions for the implementation of

love. He was seven years older than I, born before
the war, and must have felt a source of warmth, fed
to him by his memory, throughout all the time of his
misfortune…but I lacked anything of that nature, I
lacked some tiny indefinable thing, a point I failed
to find within myself, an incandescent filament;
something had been withheld from me, in a moment of carelessness or hurry that lay inconceivably
far in the past someone had forgotten to imbue me
with a faint breath, a vague thing that for anyone
else would lack all significance, a tiny tickle as from
a chance strand of hair carelessly touched for the
fraction of a second, yet a thing that could never be
made up for, and the lack of that pitiful droplet irre-
vocably condemned me to a future in hell. — This is
what I'd wanted to ask him: What is it, where does
it come from…? You must have experienced it, for
you're still alive despite your pain, your paralysis, the
smell of your purple metastases, you must know it,
how can it be installed within me? Where can I find
it, and what will happen to me if I don't, if I can't fill
the absence? Will this needle-thin drill-hole rup-
ture within me, will this barely perceptible cavity

burst to an insane, gigantic size, swallowing me up,
will it kill me…will I, doomed to be evil, end up
in the purgatorial fires? Isn't the destructive phase
of madness said to return you to the playgrounds
of your childhood; will I end up in a concentration
camp? Or in the cancer ward, amid barbed wire…or
will my hand feel nothing until it touches the lever
of the torturer's machinery? —

After summer had plunged into night, I fell
asleep after all, suddenly, as though sucked down
a vortex. But before deep sleep came, I was visited
by thoughts, startled awake again and again; in a
grinding motion they revolved beneath the surface
of my brain until, all at once, they controlled me
completely, destroying all their peripheral escape
routes in a painful, bright incineration, and I realized that they were thoughts about me, irrefutable
thoughts, appearing as truths before which every
possible appeal broke down. Years of self-deception
seemed to tear like veils, and all at once I thought I
saw myself as I really behaved with others, my real
behavior that was apparent to all.

Oh, whenever I dared to mingle among the

beautiful people on the street, in the gardens, or in the public baths, I still managed to believe I resembled them. I saw how they moved in their assurance, in their careless self-awareness, how they conversed and reposed, draped over the chairs that supported them, surrendering to a dainty hand that offered itself to them, how they danced and how laughter sprang flawless from their throats like a natural utterance of their viscera. Oh, how they solved the mathematics of all their daily tasks, how they made compelling choices whenever they went shopping, and with what unerring purpose they dressed themselves. How they used bogus words unabashedly, how they revealed even their sins and lusts to all the world with serene brows, inimitably nonchalant, certain that all was forgivable, and how their innocence remained inviolate. Inimitably...no, just not imitable by me, but I failed to realize that whenever I went out into their midst, crushed and downcast, and awkwardly tried to emulate them. I mastered keen observational skills, excruciatingly anxious to register even the hint of a mocking smile. I honed an unerring sense of hearing, but it tricked

me all the same when, in the evenings, I believed
I'd missed just one mild joke about my gaucheness,
and the suspicion made me await the next day in
heightened agitation.

But every new day that followed I saw myself in
yet a different way, yet again it seemed possible that
I could be one of them, that I could deceive them,
that they could overlook my true condition. Yes,
even overlook my boundless tension as I went into
their midst, hoping to seem at least outwardly calm.
That they wouldn't sense how utterly ensnared I was
by my anxious desire for people to like me. That I
was completely dominated by this one craving, to
be loved, and at the same time extremely concerned
not to reveal that craving to them. For I was convinced that because of this frailty I'd forfeited all
possibility of love, convinced that if they discerned
even one iota of my trepidation, they'd immediately
scorn me for it. They'd punish me with contemptu-
ous laughter because loving and being loved were
things I couldn't take for granted, things I racked
my brains over, and because I failed to casually gain
the sympathy of others: to achieve what cost them

precious little effort, what was in fact the result of non-effort; for them it meant little to eschew things they could reclaim with a wave of the hand. And in the evenings, when I was alone, I hated them for that unselfconsciousness, while knowing that since I wanted their love, they must never find out this hatred. No, they must never learn that I was in hell, that far from moving in their radiance I was absent, that I led a secret life, that in the black nights I huddled in smoke-filled dens brooding over grimy papers, in the foul-smelling sequestration of my hiding places I saw more and more vividly how I grew into a giant bestial spider that clung to its filth, chewing its cud of toxic letters amid convulsive mutterings. A monster with putrefaction written in the crannies of its skin as hectic red blotches, with uric acid drying and itching on its pate, a madness no longer stoppable as damp tufts of hair began painlessly detaching themselves. The freak who stubbed out his cigarettes in the spaces between his toes to deaden the oozy moistening itch that broke out again and again...that finally drove me out into the night, where I roamed through the most unsavory of all the ravaged spots on the hateful margins of town. Just so that I could sleep, so that tomorrow I wouldn't be so deathly pale, so that tomorrow I might be loved, if only I pretended well enough.

But I couldn't fall asleep, and thinking about the man I really was made me feel the repeated lashes of a whip that instantly inflamed my senses...all my limbs were still slumbering, incapable of resistance, but my wide-awake consciousness blazed like a torch. I was the hell-dweller who had put out his eyes, I who could perceive no real person but myself, I who thought of myself alone, thus gradually losing the ability to see...the females were already invisible to me...soon I'd be so far gone that I'd no longer see myself...in a fit of resignation I fell asleep. Never, I told myself, under these circumstances I could never be loved; this conclusion satisfied me and I was filled by a fatal calm, again and again my thoughts found their way to sleep. I yearned for nothing more fervently than for my mother to return, to be ashamed of me, curse me, treat me with contempt; this at last, so I hoped, would force me to become the Other who could think of himself from within, and thus look outward with fewer impediments. Which might mean that he still had a chance…the Other, that is…but without a chance I fell asleep.

The images in the ensuing dream were so vivid that for a long time afterward I wondered how I could have forgotten them. I'd forgotten the riddle's solution…it seemed I'd fallen asleep at the start of a very long ride and not woken up until I reached my destination, so that the entire immoderate length of the journey appeared to have vanished from my life. And yet, I told myself, something had happened on this ride…I suspected that I'd gotten out at some point, at some random stop, where something had happened to me. But I didn't know what it was; it had just been a sign that soon, perhaps only a few days from now, misfortune would strike me. And I told myself that I might have been able to avert it if only I hadn't gone back to sleep on the second half of the ride, after that forgotten stop. During that midway halt I'd been transported to a different reality, and perhaps a crucial part of the impending misfortune would be the inability to invoke the reality I'd experienced before it. — And even in my dream I'd been asleep: I was lying in bed and suddenly woke up because I thought I heard a voice. As always, it began with a harsh voice ordering me to get up, which I obeyed at once…quite possibly also doing so in reality…with the immediate knowledge that all resistance was pointless. Then the voice commanded me…unnecessarily, it seemed to me, for I felt I knew what I had to do…to lift up my nightshirt, and as always in this dream, the coarse, commanding tone rang with a mixture of amusement and revulsion: amusement that reminded me of an old popular song military bands belted out whose refrain included that same command, a song that had been played in concentration camps while prisoners were flogged; and a certain disgust that had to stem from the ludicrous sight of my filthy, sweaty nightshirt. I knew what would happen, it would be less painful than it seemed at first: with cool workmanlike hands whose movements betrayed neither fastidiousness nor gentleness, the man placed around my genitals a sturdy rope made into a noose, unclean and frayed, as thick as a finger, like a rope for trussing a sow, and the noose was narrowed with a jerk, unerringly achieving the ideal tightness a hairbreadth beneath the pain threshold. I couldn't tell whether I'd been commanded to come along; the rope tautened, and I followed without a word, the man having deftly knotted his end of the rope to the belt that clasped his dark uniform jacket at the hips. Whenever words or thoughts distracted me, I was dragged on by force...for instance, I wondered why this man had painted his fingernails bright red. After taking a closer look at the back about six feet ahead of me, I realized that the uniform clothed a broad-shouldered, unusually burly woman, a woman wearing a tightly fitting skirt that skimmed her gleaming black boots and tautened around the short, striding legs; after this view of the woman's unapproachable back I should by rights have woken up, but this time I was dragged on through a dream that moved across wide, poorly lit squares where I could make out nothing but damply gleaming cobblestones. Now I could barely feel my genitals beneath the nightshirt that draped ludicrously over the rope; only when I hesitated for a moment and the noose was pulled tight with an impatient, even brutal jerk did I realize I could still feel pain; I quickly stumbled onward, suddenly sensing that things were turning serious. — Stop, please…stop, I wanted to cry, but I had extraordinary trouble finding my voice again. Where am I being taken, I wanted to ask the woman, and who am I dealing with here?—My language seemed to have died in my throat, but at that very moment the woman turned around with a smile on her broad, rather coarse face—an expression of indulgence paired with slight resignation, evidently due to my dim-witted question. She drew herself up proudly, her feet, solidly shod in tight officer's boots, planted slightly apart, with both thumbs hooked onto her belt, and her elbows held slightly akimbo so that the black cloth of the uniform jacket strained over her big, high breasts. — Are you taking me to the barracks…? — She ignored my question. Koch, she introduced herself, I'm Ilse Koch, the gentleman must have heard my name before… — Oh yes, yes of course I know you, I cried, my tone submissive, but vibrating with a kind of joyful astonishment. — She stared at me a while longer, and I grew increasingly worried that without noticing it I might get an erection under my nightshirt. — Come with me, I know what you want…with this command she yanked me toward her, her face suddenly transformed into a malevolent, petulant mask. I hurried forward, following the tight-stretched rope that formed a line to her waist; she strode swift and unperturbed, and I heard her hobnailed boot soles slam on the pavement as though to strike sparks. — At one point I shuddered, fearing the woman might elude me, and I began to feel a colossal anxiety. But the very thought seemed to precipitate what I feared: she vanished indeed, a few more steps took her into the lustrous moonlight; backlit, her silhouette blurred and finally turned invisible, and the houses at the end of the square vanished along with her; the radiance I had been running toward suddenly seemed transformed into a gray, foggy dawn in whose light everything was fathomless and hollow. I knew that the stick had not rapped the garret floor tonight, but all the same I was about to wake up, and my regret knew no bounds.

Or perhaps I was awake already; lamplight

burned in my eyes, I'd woken in the chair, contorted and broken in the cage of a posture the chair had forced upon me. Thirst had made me burst out sweating, exhaustion had jolted me out of my sleep, summer's thick night air seemed to flow in through the window, though the window was closed…light made me moonstruck, but it was the light of the lamp beneath which I was putrefying. And something tore at me, some kind of rheumatic pain, as though coarse, unclean threads were pulling through my flesh; my upper body, lying on the table, on the slimy oilcloth, had been wrenched around as if by an artillery explosion, and with eyes wide open I stared into the burning lamp. My field of vision seemed crossed by myriad intersecting black lines, my vision was gridded by those lines, as if all the time I'd been asleep I'd been staring through a grate into a brighter space above me, and the outline of the bars had inscribed themselves deep onto my retinas. — Of course it was the alcohol that had hurled me down onto this table, as always it was the alcohol that so maliciously halved and corrupted my gaze. I couldn't recall when I'd imbibed the vast quantities of alcohol it took to do that. I lacked the courage to poison myself with hard liquor; instead I swallowed enormous quantities of inferior, brass-colored beer, which had a devious, insidiously addling effect on my mind. But this was precisely the effect I thought best suited to my unstable psyche. The beer made me bitter and nasty, it filled me with greasy, maudlin stoicism, tears ran down my cheeks, seeming to calm me, though their hypocritical source was an envy of all that was human. It calmed me to think I was sitting beneath life…staring up from underneath into the life I myself could not start living: this thought simultaneously unsettled and calmed me; my life, I suddenly knew, had been left behind in the body of my mother, but she wasn't here…I could only stare up into the life above me, through an iron square, observing the life of the cripple luminously putrefying above me…his corrosive moonshine dripped through the grate onto my face…one last time—no one was left to hold the pot under him—he had pissed himself in dying… no, he hadn't rapped his stick tonight, he couldn't any longer, no matter how loudly I'd bellowed my love up at him. And my bellowing had made me insatiably thirsty; finally rising, falling all over myself, I stumbled to the water tap…poisoned, I was poisoned…but it was as though instead of the usual black-brown water the tap emitted the sound of dark letters, in whose evil stench I dried out even more. Where was I…? Suddenly I imagined I was in an ancient, hideously dry, puritanical place, in a desert-like vacuum, enclosed by an aura of petrified asceticism that had been forced upon me, while all around me the walls I could not reach, the bloated, grinning walls oozed the oil of life… Didn't I suddenly find myself in the depths of a basement that hadn't been aired for fifty years, one of the basements I knew from my previous women's factory, whose damp underground cells I'd searched in senseless, panicked obsession in order to discover some kind of *secret*…whenever, that is, the perpetual state of hopelessness became unbearable, the state arising from the fact that no woman's foot ever stepped on the grate above me…oh, the basements to which I descended when my endless anxiety over the possibility of desire began to bore me to death, down to find a safe place to masturbate, penetrating deeper and deeper into hellish levels of the catacombs, into the labyrinth over which the former ammunition factory loomed. — And with that, I thought, I'm describing my life, my life with all its undergrounds, basement cells, underfloors, underpinnings; I'm finally putting a name to it, and perhaps by so doing I'm finally acknowledging it...but as always when that thought crossed my mind, I was too drunk to accept it. — *The Enemy is Listening!*—as on many of the doors in the factory's half-forgotten underground facilities, this sign hung on the iron door of my basement where the molds were kept, ancient, barely legible, nearly rusted away... It seemed to me that in my dream I'd been forcefully and brutally dragged back into the old basement, where I was held captive and separated from the women. Far above me I heard the nerve-shattering noise of the artillery shells being lathed. Shells, shells, a host of shells lined up neatly in handy crates, each shell with the appearance of a bulging reddish-yellow glans, stiff pricks, shells, shells, homosexual shells on pricks of banana-colored brass that had all passed through the gentle hands of the women prisoners who worked above me in that noise that pulverized my mind...metal-hard pricks in the females' oil-soft hands: I, in my basement, was shut out from it all. And ultimately I was shut out from the depraved desire which the sight of those shells might spark in the women's heads, and which the gentle caresses of their love-spoiled hands communicated to the appalling organs as they stood them up twenty units to a package; and the message of this desire was: *Death to men.*

I had trouble falling asleep again; when I woke up I realized, as I so often did, that I was essentially outside of my four walls yet again. Yes, yet again I'd drifted away from myself...I hardly ever managed to make contact with myself. How, I asked, how are you supposed to do that, to find contact with yourself...practically speaking?

Surely not by bowing to the descriptions of you by others, which are often as cruel as can be.

Surely, then, by providing your own description, a description meant for your own gaze, and thus for the world outside your window...a wanted poster.

The world outside my window lacks that gaze that is mine, so I'd sometimes told myself.

But I'd had to realize that I was no one. — I didn't know whether I existed; the fact of my birth had been kept secret from me. They kept it secret to punish me, for I hadn't turned out to be the thing they'd hoped to bestow upon the world. Yes, I'd made the mistake of having myself be born, having myself be raised by the state and its pedagogy, by pedagogy and its state—I'd practically volunteered for it—but then I turned out differently. And so I had to be nullified, voided; there was neither a womb nor a pedagogy nor a state for the creature I'd become. I didn't even have a name to lay claim to. If I wanted to start describing the world, my town for instance, the way I saw it through my eyes, I first had to engender myself, and had to do so again with each new attempt at a description. But in the unequaled fiasco of my development, neither the pedagogues nor the state had found it worthwhile to instruct me in the technical details of the progenitive act. When at last, by chance, I learned them myself, I began—my right fist forming a visual symbol that referenced this act—to rush around town, waving my lower arm to sling this symbol through the air, to make it absolutely clear to everyone that I'd resolved to engender my *I* once again. In so doing, I made a pledge, a pledge to my pedagogues: Let me do it just once, so that I can finally become *I*. — And at the same time I made a pledge to the state: If I become *I*, if I am able to do the same thing as my mother with her phallus, I'll be just like you, and thus I'll be the way you want me. I'll be a swine, an old goat, a patriarch, an officer, a toolmaker. If you let me, just once, I'll leave the trash heaps of my own free will, I'll never be a pornographer again, I'll forego my revenge. I'll forget the state's attempt to extirpate my gender by keeping my capacity for procreation secret; yes, I'll accept it, I'll forego procreating, I'll never try to engender anything but myself. But they refused to believe that I wanted to forget, they wouldn't even open their institution's gates for me.

I'd made a serious mistake, I hadn't pledged to keep engendering their idea—the idea that desire was permissible only as a gift from the state—no, I'd merely pledged to engender myself. And in so doing

I forgot that I'd been recognized as an innate evil.

Vulgar desperation. My thoughts raged, raged, but there was no answer...those three raps of the crutch on the ceiling above me, in the syllabic rhythm of the three words on the wall by the trash cans, never came. — You are dead. Your eyes have given up describing...should I follow you? The pale yellow syrup I'd vomited while sleeping in the inert light of the ceiling lamp that joined my lips to the filthy tablecloth, the fungus spreading beneath my hair, the crust that covered my tongue each evening after I slept away the day that I moistened with the water dripping brown from the tap, then coughed black letters, crosses, jagged medallions into the sink: this, from now on, would be the material for describing my *I*. For describing a darkness-soaked stream of summers, light gridded by swarms of black type, a myriad of glowing filament *E*s that the lamp branded into my pupils. — Could I reach the trash heaps before the night was over, hurrying to huddle there amid the damp, hairy rubbish, to await the morning among nasty curs and copulating rats so that I could be the first to pounce, chance permitting, on some blurred piece of paper, a page documenting my sexuality, to use that awful word…? Probably not.

No, I knew it would be reckless of me to leave the house. — I did it anyway…warily I peered around to see if dogs or policemen were roaming near the house, but heard nothing, the full moon dripped down a stearin glimmer in which everything was deathly still. I hurried to reach the trash cans; from one of them I'd once dragged a corked bottle, still half full, which I took for a bottle of champagne. I'd given up on the paper…I'd try to reach my goal without it…in cases like mine, I told myself, hope is an almost unbearable cowardice, an extraordinary compromise tempting you to set nothing in motion ever again, to sit in your own filth and wait until that hope transpires. When in fact there's only one hope: the hope of becoming unbearable. Without the hope of someone to help you bear things… You must still have had that hope, my friend, up there in your garret room. I always envied you for your bearability, but that was likely a mistake. The three words whose rhythm you produced with three raps in response to my cry are still scribbled on the wall in obscene chalk letters, showing that I'm in the right place. In our fantasies, my friend, we've long since adopted the name behind those words, I said with a peculiar grin. — And as I spoke I quietly opened, with less effort than I'd expected, a gap of about half a yard between the last two cans in the row. In this gap I sat down on the pavement with my legs splayed, my back pressed against the last container still with the rest of the row, quite straight, and then I pulled the last can close to my body. I pulled it as tightly as possible into the semicircle of my outspread legs, took a deep breath, and tugged once more at the can, a final jerk that wedged my lower body in place, so that I was set almost seamlessly between the two containers' greasy zinc walls. Then I fumbled my genitals out of my pants, and with cautious balance I leaned my penis against the wall of the trash can that rose in front of me; it took me several tries to succeed, it went awry, despite the inscription on the wall above my head I couldn't manage to simulate an erection, and finally contented myself with having the tip of my penis touch the zinc, shrinking from the night-cool metal. Eager to keep the plot of this immolation moving, I'd forgotten to take the half- or three-quarters-filled champagne bottle out of the trash can. I did so now, sat back down again as before, and placed the bottle just below the waist of my opened trousers, right on the palm-sized patch of skin where blond hairs sprouted. The slender green neck topped by the white plastic cork reared magnificently, somehow reminding me of the anatomical sketches we'd passed back and forth under our desks during political education sessions in my army days. I'd already sampled the bottle with my nose, and there was no doubt that it held gasoline, gasoline that had to be virtually if not completely unsalable; I carefully recorked the bottle and pondered what to do. I resorted to an old habit; first slowly and with feeling, then more and more rapidly and intensely, I began to masturbate; this time, in a deviation from routine, albeit a small one, I did so with my entire fist, closing it cautiously at first, then tighter and tighter; the neck of the bottle seemed to be wet on the outside as well, so it went effortlessly, indeed with wonderful ease; I felt the glass of the bottle start to warm, and paused just twice to wipe the sweat from my brow. It's possible, I knew, for rapid warming to bring champagne bottles to ejaculation; if the bottle were heated enough, the powerful orgasm of the fermenting champagne would send the cork flying into my face...but despite the utmost exertions I couldn't manage it, my hand slackened, and with resignation I ceased my movements.

My fate was written by the confused bus rides that blurred together in my memory... Suddenly, sitting there wedged in on the sidewalk, I was overcome by a familiar feeling: it was as if I were sitting jammed inside a bus, amid densely packed fleshy bodies that pushed against me in bitter resistance, with hatred in fact, pressing against my aching, twisted thighs...evidently I'd managed to snatch the last free seat away from them...all that was missing was the rhythmic juddering of the vehicle that had persistently given me erections in my too-tight trousers. The various spans of time that bus had traversed with me inside became stretches of space in recollection, different spaces which had nothing to do with one another, and I no longer knew how often I'd ridden that route in the period I was recalling, how often I'd gotten off, gotten back on, fallen asleep again, been thrown out again from the warm interior of that swaying box filled with pungent smells…in fact, the green exhalations of the lacerated vinyl upholstery, soaked by the sweat of so many crotches, reminded me of the smell of the females. I'd only encountered it before as the burned smell of melted plastic that floated over the waters in the pressing shop. And I truly felt I'd been shut up in a quivering vagina: the bus, the interior with its inner movements, pushing, contracting, was a gigantic symbol for a vagina…it wasn't driving, it was falling at a breakneck speed that took away my breath and my weight, sinking through all the different days and weeks only to dump me implacably in the town of my birth, suddenly outside its body's moist interior, cut off, and the orangish, urine-colored bus hobbled on to birth another litter, exhausted, voided, but undeterred.

I got to my feet and walked away, nervous as a hunted man. I tried to recall the feeling I'd had when the pressing shop still awaited me—the pressing shop…I felt as though I'd lost my mother—but all that came to mind was an old project: I'd wanted to write a love story with a tragic ending. It was pointless to search for old, lost texts in order to tell it; the words themselves contained the necessary materials, and the story's tragic ending could be created from inside myself as well, from the material of my existence and the language that went along with it. This country, I believed, offered plenty of tools for the purpose; the subsoil of this country was practically groaning with suppressed descriptions.

Indeed, fittingly enough, there seemed to be plenty of tragic material, material of virtually intolerable absurdity, tragedy that burst with absurdity. — It had gotten to the point that I spent several days collecting old women's clothes from the trash heaps, painstakingly storing the slimy, moldy rags in a small cardboard suitcase; I meant to begin a new life with them; in my physical and mental degeneration I really was thinking about a new life to follow the death of my old life, however hard it was to admit it to myself. My thoughts—making a travesty of the human mental functions—went something like this: A moment would inevitably come when my descriptions of myself as a man would break down, and this would be the moment to seize. A moment in which I could ridicule the symbolism of my male descriptions, which had long since turned into an associative free-for-all, and whose style was increasingly deteriorating. Descriptions, I said to myself, have this peculiarity: when they describe something that has a processual character, they arrest the thing at some point that's sure to be premature, preventing the process from continuing any further; and for that reason they are reactionary. — Reactionary, I said aloud, walking onward. — Reactionary, I repeated, mimicking myself. — The process of free association often prompted the resounding speeches that I delivered to myself, as I mentioned earlier, while wandering through town at night or walking back to town from the garbage dumps, trying to drown out the night bus as it roared past, to spare my consciousness the anxiety-inducing thought that some essence of femininity lingered inside that vehicle. — A hard-core reactionary, I yelled, yes, a real

hard-core reactionary. This phrase gave me pause…
the adjective *hard* suggests a phallic symbol…and
thus our republic's ideology unwittingly credits the
foe with considerable virility. It would be no wonder
if the females had absconded in that direction.

Preoccupied with these thoughts, I had finally
arrived in front of the police station.

But no, I thought now, *hard-core* just means
obstinate, intransigent…words I'd had some experience with, because I'd been under constant threat
of reform school, court proceedings, the workhouse,
ever since elementary school. — If you wanted to
make the word *reactionary* into a phallic symbol,
you'd have to add the word *bottle*, perhaps mean-
ing a bottle in which everything has hardened,
which doesn't react, even under great heat. Pen-
sively I regarded the champagne bottle I'd brought
along, I shook my head, set it carefully on the curb,
and sat down beside it. — Champagne, I thought,
fizzy champagne…that would turn my perfidy into
beauty. As I had too little money to donate an ac-
ceptable sum to the state, perhaps the champagne
bottle would do. Really, I could grab it by the neck,

whirl it around my head and offer it up to them with the velocity of a grenade. Oh, the blue glitter of the opaquely gleaming windows in the night. — And wouldn't the gift of that bottle also compensate for my screaming…my terrible screams outside the closed police station, my attempt at a confrontation. And what had I screamed, anyway, was it Zola's accusatory word from the Dreyfus Affair, so famous despite its absurdity…? Idiotic though it was, at some point I had screamed that word. — Or I'd screamed the word *grenade…grenade*…at least it sounded like that. — I recalled that during my repeated shouts the lights had gone out in the few still-lit windows of the police station. As though I weren't supposed to see…as though I weren't supposed to know behind which windows the police were still at work. — *Grenade*…all at once I felt that the word was a woman's name. *Grenade, bazooka*… these really did remind me of women's names. — I leaped up: the champagne bottle over there on the curb, what did it remind me of? The womb simulacrum in the trash can, women's clothes dangling from the trash cans, skirts I put my hands up while calling women's names, women's names that made the police turn their lights out.

Or did that mean that someone in this town was listening to me...one single person...or perhaps even an entire police force?—I laughed mockingly: Where were they then, and where were the women? I looked at the bottle with renewed interest; a very tempting thought seemed concealed inside it.

The moment had come to halt the process; this was the moment to change things. Henceforth it was not I who needed to be newly described, but the females, since I could no longer find them. Yes, they needed to be newly pieced together from the materials available to me. What I could see were descriptions of women from literature, from the newspapers...myriads of them, whole insect swarms of black type that described women; wasn't I completely shrouded in them, hosts of flies, gigantic alphabets of midges, black mosquitoes, locusts? But I felt I must forswear what already existed, for these descriptions had been made by men...it wasn't enough to single one of them out, to picture it to myself, to call it up before my mind's eye, as the vivid phrase goes, in the hope that its figure and its soul would come to a standstill before me. I'd just end up falling back on those old prototypes again: my mother perhaps, the Virgin Mary, Karl Marx, or maybe Kaspar Hauser. No, perhaps I'd have to adopt a female gaze first. From one of my scavenger hunts in the trash heaps I'd taken home a huge yellow woman's hat, and I recalled that my mother, or one of the women from my distant past, had worn a hat like that in the summer, if not that very same one. I recalled how I looked up to stare into a circular yellow firmament, like a second sun that encompassed the entire horizon, and how I turned dizzy, how I lost all my earthly weight, and almost thought I was flying into those yellow-flaming heights, so that, out of balance, I had to cling to the woman's knees... perhaps this was the gaze I had to recapture.

And yet they must be made from earth. Hadn't they, just like me, been made from earth at one time? Didn't they all contain the same glues that flowed from me—breath, mucus, tears—that flowed out to turn to earth once more? Didn't all the sickness and putrefaction clinging to me simply mark the beginning of my transformation back into earth, and wasn't this so for *all human beings*; mustn't the females be made from earth as well? No rib of mine was necessary, anyway. All the things that escaped me every day, those substances already foreign to me, substances turning invisible…spittle, semen, shit… blood, dandruff, pox, scabs, sweat, filth, and the stale atmosphere that fled my lungs, what was all that but earth, and needn't the females be described using the same things, couldn't they too be created only from earthly descriptions? Didn't the walking grave that was me contain, from the outset, all the means for doing so? How could I dream up a material that was theirs without thinking of my own material? I could bequeath them my fingernails, my teeth if need be, but they had to have souls that were different from mine. Perhaps their souls had to be begged from a female deity, who was Gaia, Earth. — And I would call these creatures the *females*, rather than *women*, flying in the face of prohibition, because it sounded more animal, more earthly. — But their souls might need to be described in much the same way as their hair. Surging and soft, a torrent that began to turn dark in the rain.

And suddenly I knew the place where the females had truly been present. Throughout my childhood I'd played with the idea of their souls. Throughout my childhood I'd unconsciously been searching for those souls. Again and again I'd expected to suddenly find them, all at once to see them lying in an unlooked-for room in the concentration camp barracks. Suddenly to stand before the wild tumultuous mounds of their hair, into which I could sink my hands, into which I could wade. Oh, if only I could have plunged one single time into the darkness of their souls, they'd never have vanished from me, they'd have continued to be present for me.

Yes, I felt I must describe the females who had lived in the torment and the simple solidarity of these barracks, where they were called *females*, because *women* staffed the guard details. That was where that honorific was invented: the females.

And when I stood outside my town, trying to recall myself to myself, those long rows of females came to mind; on the very evening of my birth they must have been herded past on the street below after leaving the factory, past the corner below where the long rows of trash cans now gleamed. Driven to the camp that began at the end of our street. And that evening might have marked my first awareness of them, with yellow evening heavens enabling me to fly, my memory of those ceaseless dragging steps, the muteness of their ranks, the weary wandering and coughing of those ceaseless rows of females.

And being a man, and not of their kind, I tried to get in through an old door. It was a door that had seemingly never been opened—smoothly painted over with yellow-brown paint, even the keyhole had been painted shut—a side door to the labyrinth of garret rooms where the cripple was ensconced by his window. I was unable to open that side door and slink in softly, inaudibly; I knew there were old closets there, old chests in which the females of our house kept unserviceable things, former possessions and bundles of old documents. Perhaps the lost pornography I'd sought in the trash was hidden there as well...but mainly I hoped to find my father's old letters from the front, which—it was not completely impossible—might contain some mention of me. And if it were in reply to a letter from my mother, it would prove that a woman had once acknowledged my existence… Now that the cripple's soul had long since taken flight through regal yellow skies, he would no longer hinder me from searching the garret for a piece of evidence I needed to write my tragic love story: now I could try to open the door.

Picking up the champagne bottle, I was about to leave when suddenly I felt as though I had an endless distance to go, as though a vast stretch of road lay ahead of me; suddenly I doubted whether my feet could carry me all the way to my goal. All the way to town…no, it seemed I hadn't reached town yet, it lay far below me, over it a full moon cast a pale dome of light…it lay below me, and I saw myself on the trash heaps, trying to penetrate the light with my gaze…I was ancient, grown old amid that immense accumulation of trash that had given birth to my town…my feet would barely carry me if I tried to return to the town now, but I couldn't let myself think about that, couldn't let myself think that my dismissal was irreversible; I had to stride forward, heedless, with nothing but my last hope, ah no, lacking all hope, I had to stride toward the miracle, if need be crawl toward the miracle.

You females...who mustn't be called that anymore...isn't this the only explanation for your condition: that some unheard-of sensitization of my eyes has made you invisible to me? That I am a man transformed into the tiniest of things, and before me, before my eyes' insect-like sensitivity, a monstrous metaphor is manifesting itself? Am I not simply the chosen one, chosen through some terrible mistake, who persists in God's great petrified lie? And isn't it clear to all that the chosen ones will be beaten? She's waiting for me in that house down there, she's waiting for her husband, her god. Should I give up at last, and transform myself into my father? Should I at last profess to being chosen...? Oh, I'll only disappoint her once again; I can't be a hundred percent her husband, nor a hundred percent her god. I'll remain the child in the ark, set adrift on all shoreless rivers, senselessly expelled. Senselessly found, taken to land, senselessly rescued

anew. And wasn't I that wanderer of the deserts, females all I succumbed to, wasn't I myself the *Moses*
my hymns were sung to? Who fell down before the
portal, who will not pass through until his death. Let
him lead the sons, and, free from envy, the halfway
father, let him cover them with his blessings when
they pass through. With him collapsed outside the
gate, while those he showed the way no longer turn
to look at him, outside the gate, that portal which
they call—hackneyed, worn-out, overstretched—by
the mythical term *the gates of paradise*. On bended
knees, unable to see with scar-covered retinas, able
only, dying, to sense the gates distantly, oh, to see the
gray light called sweet darkness recede beyond the
portal. To see it darker and darker, that is, sweeter
and sweeter, the sweeter it is the harder to attain,
more unattainable the farther the dying gaze tries
to penetrate. And nothing penetrates now but the
gaze. Do I really see this town of mine only through
the band of a cunt? Do I see nothing now but how
it blurs back there and goes soft? Unfilled void,
glimmering dim over onward-growing, swelling
forms; chameleon-colored, fish-mouth closed with

the inertia of metals flowing together. Quicksilver mushroom membranes growing together, flooded with milky serum. Until that medusa-like boundary reminds me, the blind man, that the real existence of my town can be experienced only by smell. And was it really to be found behind that cleft of flesh I saw last…behind that obscenely grimacing mouth of skin and hair formed by my half-opened eyelids? Is it down there still, behind the lashed slit of my eye that a frigid sleep now seeks to close? Would it still be discernible behind the fleetingly parted thighs of the woods? Down there in the south, my town that staged my brilliant ovulation. That spat me out in the heat of the summer, with the shudder of a thirsty cry, the slap of a blind shell landing in the mud; it was I who was born in a cloudburst of breaking green waters… My father was born to my town, and in their fear the females shuffled faster past the street corner under the window…while birth swallowed me up and throttled me, throttled, strangled, snapped at me, but finally spat me out anyway…the birth of my father mixed up its spawn, it was I it vomited out, the first raven cry it squeezed out was mine. Cursed town, I won't sing your praises with my father's prick; cursed town, I'll pour myself all over you, I'll jerk off against your walls, I…I'll pass down the sloping tracks of dead bodies between you and me, *O maman*, my sun of absentia, I won't heed the dead gods between us, I'll come closer to gaze at last into the place of my birth, into the hole of my birth, closer to gaze into my nation. Females, I'll take your fathers from you. Oh, so as to gaze at last through this blurred lens, through this grate. Oh, to press to my eye the scalding monocle of a vulva. To learn how to see, to recognize myself in you. To see the blood, your blood that has grown on inside me, in my veins' Milky Way; to see the nerves menstruating within the windings of my brain. To smell death as it begins to cover me with black spots. To see the twitching of the genius as it schemes to slip out in the fluid channel of your darkness. No, I'll wait no longer, I don't want you to hold my eyes shut forever. Not only my breath should stroke the strength of your thighs, my breath that once learned to breathe within you. My eyes want you back as well, my eyes that, through you, learned how to see.

My eyes want to press close to you. To your water plants, to the hole of your rage. To your soul's lovely core, to the cloaca with your feces. To the exploded bomb in your flesh. Down the branches of your veins…to cease comparing you to vegetative things: your hair doesn't flutter in the trees, you aren't in the flowers, nor in the fruit and vegetables that rot in the trash cans…down your hills, to cease comparing you to animal things, O she-wolf…to let the soft pulse of your senses mount in my throat at last… not to kill, only to compare you at last to human and female things, O creatress…ah, so that I no longer need to compare you with your silence, with your invisibility, with your odorlessness, with your murderous purity. Yes, your murderous purity is a dead general's vengeance. — Ah, are you finally where I can't follow you, jailer, have you finally fallen in line among the ranks, are you finally free in your silence? Oh, you've freed yourself from the word that loved me, and I'm chasing all alone through the madness of my dreams that still echo with the word your mouth spoke, your cunt spoke. And you say you can never forgive me…never forgive me…you're divorced from Jack the Ripper…you say you can't stand me any longer, but are you really free, in your carefully dosed academic silence? You needn't reveal it to me, you needn't do what you once wanted to do, before you'd freed yourself from love. — Sad labor of persuasion, as I toil, handful by handful. — I'm speaking to you as though you really were free now…and I hear you laugh, I hear you laugh long and unflagging. Your laughter drowns out the stick rapping above the ceiling of the room, faint padding footsteps through the smoke. Though your freedom may be possible in other countries, in the sight of this nation it's soaked in blood. Corpses lie between the barbed-wire barriers within sight of your wild rendezvous. Gas taps open into this freedom. The wall around your freedom is pocked with bullet holes, electric shocks lash lazy madmen in the cells of your freedom. Your freedom is paid for with the money of those left behind. It's not your fault that I was left behind, I forgot you on a long ride spent sleeping…

But I still want to come to you, come closer. Closer, to press my eye to the fluid flesh between your legs. To see at last what's at the bottom of your silence. Yes, I love you, to shut my lids. The eye in your flesh, I love you, to open my lids…to shut, to open, quick, to shut to open, oh to fly with my lids. To open your cry within you with my lids. With my lashes, my long lashes. Thoroughly bedewed by you.

My lashes, my long lashes…
See, I descend
To forget in your lap

No answer, no echo. We're no longer under cover, our hair flutters beneath the yellow sky. We've been released, females, and all that we were, released from the factory, from the country, from the camp, from life…let us be let go, wretched tools that we were, let us go silently, don't let go my hand, God in his heaven waves his hat to us.

No answer. I knew I had failed to describe the females; they were absent still, absent from this town, absent from my description. Absent like light and life in these streets…I grasped the monstrous and merciless theft of reality that had been perpetrated against me. And it grew dark around me, and dark inside me too…if, against all expectation, they had suddenly appeared now, I would no longer have been able to perceive them, they would have found no place inside me. — As if to rob even my last thought of its vitality, suddenly the lamps shone out from the dark police building, switched on one by one behind the windows of the station house. A beam of light spilling onto the street made my champagne bottle blaze on the curb by the gutter. Blaze…as though to keep a thought from leaving my head, I squeezed shut my lips and my eyelids: if the females didn't exist, then I need not exist either. I seized the bottle, uncorked it, and poured it over my head. The gasoline soaked my hair, flowed over my face, flowed down my collar, and drenched my shirt, very little gas, but enough to run slowly under my belt; my pubic hair must have taken on a loathsome oily smell. My trousers clung smoothly to my skin, the last drips of gasoline petered out on my thighs. It was enough for a torch, for a human torch right outside the police station. I searched my pockets for matches. Cursing, I rummaged through my clothes in search of matches, but I found none.

What could I do? Ring the station doorbell and ask if they had matches? I was afraid they'd guess my plan before I could carry it out. — So I didn't even have matches on me—were they in one of the pieces of women's clothing I'd tried on?—and before I reached home the gasoline would dry on my skin. I had failed as utterly as it was possible to fail, I completely lacked existence, I couldn't even look forward to an existence as a jet of flame soaring to the sky. — All the same, I suddenly had doubts, the situation was much too crazy not to have doubts after all, I could always buy matches tomorrow. Tomorrow was another day. The thought of buying matches calmed me down a bit. Amid my doubt I'd heard a menacing tone in my thoughts. Scornfully I tossed the bottle back into one of the trash cans as I passed.

Unable to stand it in town any longer, I moved to Berlin. I packed my shabby cardboard suitcase with care—the yellow summer hat was the only thing I couldn't fit—and without anyone noticing, I left my little germ cell and moved into a dilapidated building in Berlin. There, in the big city where I'd hoped to have better luck, I found work, and soon it really seemed that my diseases had withdrawn inside me; outwardly I seemed to become sleek, I even gained weight; I drank until I had a beer belly and observed my reinvigoration in the mirror. Only the sickness of my language still lingered; I sensed it distinctly, but made no attempt to put it to the test. Apart from a brief tram ride to my workplace, I barely left the house. I'd been employed by the boiler house of a large laundry, joining the crew of stokers who generated the steam used for heating and to operate the washing machines. The laundry proper was separated from the boiler room by a massive wall of yellowish concrete crowned by barbed wire; no one from the area I worked in was allowed to set foot in the laundry or have any contact with the people behind that wall, who were cut off from the outside world: the laundry was staffed by the inmates of a huge prison that abutted the laundry complex. But it was possible, I'd learned from one of my colleagues, if you were careful…infractions could lead to transferral out of the stoking unit, which was so congenial for me, or even to dismissal…to climb the fire escape to the roof of the boiler house and from there look down into the prison yard.

One Sunday morning…it was already turning cool, and the prison had to be heated even on Sundays…on a clear autumn day with a few clouds, I was strolling, bored, across the yard between the boiler house and that gigantic wall, when I heard voices. Quite close by I heard loud yells, commands, the shrilling of whistles, and even dogs barking. I knew it was the time of day when the prisoners were let out into the prison yard for their daily half hour of exercise, and on an impulse I climbed the ladder's iron rungs to the roof of the boiler house. Up on the flat roof I ducked behind a chimney and peered over the wall. What I saw I'd known about already, but suddenly I felt that I couldn't believe my eyes. The women were walking in the yard down there. Sedately, absorbed in animated chatter, the women were walking in rows of two or three, strolling in a circle, flanked by female guards with big German shepherds; they were dressed in dark-green, uniform-like woolen clothes, the institutional dress of this big women's prison; they seemed in high spirits, laughing, tossing unintelligible jokes to each other. They were young and old, stout and thin; I saw the swells of their breasts, the glide of their thighs under their skirts. I saw their hair, brown and blond hair, sometimes cut short, sometimes falling to their shoulders in waves. I tried to see their faces; I couldn't see them well, but I seemed to recognize some as harmonious, beautiful, angel-like faces. I felt that what was happening to me now had to happen as it did—I wasn't sure whether I'd seen them around Berlin as well, it didn't matter, it didn't interest me...it was here that my eyes had opened all the way, here that I saw them in reality, here that I found them once again. I saw them at a distance of perhaps twenty yards, they strolled and chatted down below, watched by their guards... women, females. I saw them and shivered; it was no hallucination, in that instant I was freed from all doubts. — I love you all, I murmured in rapture, I love you. — What words, I said with a smile, as though among these fifty or so creatures I had seen one I could really mean those words for in so brief a

time. It doesn't matter, I said, one of them will understand these three words. — And I took heart and
cried: I love you!… Aghast, I heard the cry and its
echo reverberate across the entire laundry complex.
But none of the women even looked up…I didn't
dare repeat the cry; I knew they couldn't look up if
they didn't want to betray me, but clearly they all
sensed that I was crouching, barely hidden, behind
the chimney. Several minutes passed, and suddenly I
sensed that they were giving a sign. They were giving
me a sign; several of them had thrust their thumbs
between their index and middle fingers and cautiously raised their hands to chest level, still gazing
ahead jadedly. I understood: they were giving me a
filthy sign, the filthiest one possible, they had allied
themselves with me; it was a sign aimed against the
pure State. And it also meant: wait for us…wait just
a few more years… — The sign sank down into my
innermost being, for an instant I shut my eyes in
ecstasy. But then I started, I'd heard something behind me, as though a second reply to my cry had
reached me from behind. I looked around, and in an
open window on the other side of the street, almost

exactly at my level, a man was staring over at me fixedly. I could look him straight in the eye, and I guessed it was he who had replied to me with an audible cough. I recalled that everyone in the boiler house was convinced the apartments in the buildings directly across from the prison were rented out mainly to low-ranking members of the security service, so that the prison gate and surrounding area could be under observation at all times. — Yes, yes, wait for me, he'd coughed out…a man, about my age. Quickly I climbed back down the ladder and fled into the boiler house…a shadow seemed to fall on the feather-light autumn Sunday. With a crowbar in my hand I positioned myself behind the door; a fit of trembling seized me…if he dared come after me, I'd…but the man didn't appear in the doorway, he hadn't followed me. After a while I calmed myself…I could think about the females, and soon it no longer seemed so surprising that I'd seen them once again. They had descended upon me with the glass-clear light of this bright-blue fall sky, they'd returned refulgent to my eyes. They'd been left behind inside me, with the singing and tittering of fall days that finally swept away the air of madness smoldering over the summer of my birth. Now I knew where they were to be found, I'd seen them again and preserved them in my heart; I could wait for them.

WOLFGANG HILBIG (1941–2007) was one of the major German writers to emerge in the postwar era. Though raised in East Germany, he proved so troublesome to the authorities that in 1985 he was granted permission to leave to the West. The author of over twenty books, he received virtually all of Germany's major literary prizes, capped by the 2002 Georg Büchner Prize, Germany's highest literary honor.

ISABEL FARGO COLE is a U.S.-born, Berlin-based writer and translator. Her translations include Wolfgang Hilbig's *The Sleep of the Righteous*, *"I," Old Rendering Plant* (for which she received the Helen and Kurt Wolff Translator's Prize), and *The Tidings of the Trees*. She has also been the recipient of a prestigious PEN/Heim Translation Grant, and her novel *Die grüne Grenze* was a finalist for the 2018 Preis der Leipziger Buchmesse.